We hope you enjoy this book.
Please return or renew it by the due date.
You can renew it at **www.norfolk.gov.uk/libraries** or by using our free library app. Otherwise you can phone **0344 800 8020** - please have your library card and pin ready.
You can sign up for email reminders too.

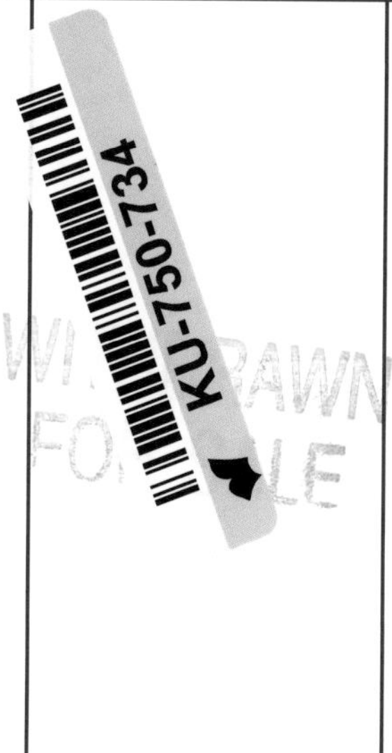

SWEPT INTO THE TYCOON'S WORLD

SWEPT INTO THE TYCOON'S WORLD

CARA COLTER

MILLS & BOON

First published in Great Britain 2018
by Mills & Boon, an imprint of HarperCollins*Publishers*
1 London Bridge Street, London, SE1 9GF

Large Print edition 2018

ISBN: 978-0-263-07449-9

MIX
Paper from
responsible sources
FSC www.fsc.org
FSC® C007454

This book is produced from independently certified FSC™ paper to ensure responsible forest management. For more information visit www.harpercollins.co.uk/green.

Printed and bound in Great Britain
by CPI Group (UK) Ltd, Croydon, CR0 4YY

To Kymber,
the man my daughter has given her heart to.

CHAPTER ONE

"WHO IS THAT?" Chelsea's whisper was breathless.

Bree Evans shot her young assistant an exasperated look. "You've got to stop it. We were asked at the briefing not to gawk at the celebrities. It's part of our agreement to provide sample products and a display for this event. To be strictly professional. No staring. No autographs. No—"

Chelsea, unaware, or uncaring, that she was jeopardizing Bree's big break, was not paying the least bit of attention to her boss. Instead she was standing completely frozen, a neatly gift-wrapped box of Kookies for All Occasions' Love Bites in her hand. Bree followed her gaze, looking toward the outside door that led into the foyer area of the concert hall, where they were setting up.

Oh, no.

"Who *is* that?" Chelsea whispered again.

Oh, no. Had she said it out loud?

He was everything Bree remembered, only more. She had not seen him, in person, anyway, for six years. Though it hardly seemed possible, in that time his *presence* had multiplied. He had lost any hint of boyish slenderness, and the gorgeous lines of his face had settled into maturity. His dark brown hair, which she remembered as untamed, touching his collar and sweeping across his forehead, was now cut short and neatly groomed, as befit his position.

"It's Brand Wallace," Bree said carefully. She positioned herself with her back to the doorway he was coming through. Her heart was beating way too fast. Good grief. Her palms were sweating.

"Like in *Braveheart*?" Chelsea gasped.

"That was Mel Gibson," Bree explained with what was left of her patience. "Gibson *played* the part of William Wallace—he *wasn't* William Wallace."

Still, even though she didn't want to, Bree understood why Brand would make her young assistant think of brave hearts. There was something about him, and always had been—a way of moving with supreme grace and confidence that suggested a warrior, a man who was certain in his own strength and courage and capabilities.

Chelsea was still totally distracted. "I have never seen a more stunning example of the male of the species. Never."

Despite ordering herself not to, Bree slid another careful look at the doorway. She had to give Chelsea that. Brand Wallace was a stunning example of the male species!

He'd stopped just inside the double glass doors, his head tilted toward Shelley Grove, organizer of the Stars Come Out at Night, a charity gala to help fund the construction of a new wing for Children's Hospital.

Shelley had her hand cozily on his arm and was beaming up at him. He was steel, and women were magnets drawn to him.

Though the room was beginning to fill with well-known celebrities, many of whom were in

Vancouver—"Hollywood North," as it was sometimes called—filming television series and movies, he stood out from all of them.

Even surrounded by some of the world's most dazzling people, there was something about him that was electric. It sizzled in the air around him, sensual and compelling.

He was in a sports jacket that, by the cut, hang and fit, was obviously designer. It showed the breadth of his shoulders, the power in him. White shirt—no doubt silk—and no tie. The shirt was tucked into dark jeans that clung to the hard lines of his thighs.

He was as fit and muscular, as outdoorsy-looking, as he had been when he'd worked as a summer student for her dad's landscaping company.

Brand made the extremely famous actor, who was standing a short distance away from him, look small and very, very ordinary.

"I'm sure I know who he is," Chelsea said, her tone mulling. "I've seen him in something. *Warriors of the New Age?* No, I know all of them.

Maybe that new series. You know the one? Where the lady time-travels and the gorgeous guy—"

"He's not an actor," Bree said. "Chelsea, please put the cookies out. We only have twenty minutes until the official start time and I—"

She had to what? Leave, obviously. Before he saw her.

"But I know who he is," Chelsea said. "I'm sure of it." She unwillingly turned back to emptying the cookie-filled boxes, her body angled sideways so she could keep casting glances his way.

"You probably saw him on the cover of *City* magazine," Bree said. "That's why you feel as if you know who he is. Could you put a row of Devilishly Decadent at the end of the display?"

"Brand Wallace," Chelsea announced, way too loudly. "The billionaire! You're right! *City* had him on the cover. I couldn't turn around without seeing that glorious face on every newsstand! I don't usually buy it, but I did. He founded an internet start-up company that went insane with success—"

Bree shot a look to the doorway. Apparently he

had heard Chelsea yelling his name like a teenager who had spotted her rock-star idol. He was casting a curious look in their direction.

Bree did not want him to see her. She particularly did not want him to see her in her Kookies outfit. She and Chelsea were both wearing the uniforms she had designed, and Chelsea had sewn. Until precisely three minutes ago, she had been proud of how she had branded her company.

Kookies sold deliciously old-fashioned cookies with a twist: unexpected flavors inside them, and each different type claimed to hold its own spells.

And so the outfits she and Chelsea wore were part sexy witch, part trustworthy grandmother. They both had on granny glasses, berets shaped like giant cookies, and their aprons—over short black skirts and plain white blouses—had photos of her cookies printed on them, quilted to make them look three-dimensional. It was all so darn *cute*.

Somehow she did not want the man her father had convinced to escort her to her senior prom to see her as cute. Or kooky. She certainly did not want him to see her with a giant cookie on her head!

In fact, she did not want Brand Wallace to see her at all. He belonged to another time and another place. A time when she had still believed in magic. A place that had felt as if her world would always be safe.

She shot another glance at the doorway. He was still looking in their direction—she could see he was trying to extricate himself from the conversation with Shelley.

"He's coming this way," Chelsea sighed. "How's my hair?"

Out of the corner of her eye, Bree saw Chelsea flicking her hair. She also saw there was an emergency exit just a little behind and to the left of their table. For some reason, it felt imperative to get out of there. And out of the apron. And the beret. Especially the beret.

It was trying to remove both at once that proved dangerous. She was twisting the apron over her head and taking off the beret with it, when, too late, she saw the corner of a box of Little Surprise cookies that was jutting out from under her display table. At the last second she tried to get her foot over it and failed.

The toe of her shoe caught on the box, and it caught the leg of the table, which folded. Apron and beret twisted around her neck, she had to make a split-second decision whether to save the cookies or herself. The cookies, which represented so much hard work, and her future—being invited to participate in this event was a huge coup for her company—won.

She dove under a cascade of Spells Gone Wrong boxes, which fell on her, one by one, until she was very nearly buried in them.

Really, it was a slow-motion and silent disaster, except for the fact she had managed to break the fall of the delicate cookies.

The incident probably would have gone completely unnoticed if Chelsea had not started shrieking dramatically.

And then he was there, moving the avalanche of boxes gently out of the way to reveal Bree underneath them. He held out a hand to her.

"Miss, are you—"

He stopped. He stared at her.

She blinked where she was lying on the floor, covered in boxes, and remembered. She remembered his eyes, the glorious deep brown of them, warm as dark-roasted coffee. She remembered that very same tilt of his mouth, something faintly sardonic and unconsciously sexy in it.

She remembered the *feeling* of his gaze on her, and a forbidden warmth unfolded in her that made her feel boneless.

"Bree?" he said, astounded.

She heard Chelsea's cluck of astonishment.

"Breanna Evans," he said slowly, softly, his voice a growl of pure sensuality that scraped the nape of her neck. And then his hand, strong and heated, closed around hers and he pulled her to her feet, the cookie boxes, which she had sacrificed her escape to save, scattering. His grasp was unintentionally powerful, and it carried her right into the hard length of him. She had been right. The shirt was silk. For a stunned moment she rested there, feeling his heat and the pure heady male energy of him heating the silk to a warm, liquid glow. Feeling what she had felt all those years ago.

As if the world was full of magical possibilities.

She put both hands on the broadness of his chest, and shoved away from him before he could feel her heart, beating against him, too quickly, like a fallen sparrow held in a hand.

"Brand," she said, she hoped pleasantly. "How are you?"

He studied her without answering.

She straightened the twisted apron. Where was the beret? It was kind of stuck in the neckline of the apron and she yanked it out, and then shoved it in the oversize front pocket, where it created an unattractive bulge.

"You're all grown up," he said, in a way that made her blush crimson.

"Yes," she said, stiffly, "People do tend to do that. Grow up."

She ordered herself not to look at his lips. She looked. They were a line of pure sexy. The night of her prom she had hoped for a good-night kiss.

But he hadn't thought she was grown up then. Did it mean anything that he saw her as grown up now?

Of course it did not! Chances of her tasting those lips were just as remote now as they had been then. He was a billionaire, looking super-suave and sophisticated, and she was a cookie vendor in a bulging apron. She nearly snorted at the absurdity of it.

And the absurdity that she would still even *think* of what those lips would taste like.

But she excused her momentary lapse in discipline. There wasn't a woman in the entire room who wasn't thinking of that! Chelsea's interest, from the first moment she had laid eyes on him, had made it clear Brand Wallace's sex appeal was as potent as ever.

"You know each other?" Chelsea asked, her voice a miffed squeak, as if Bree had kept state secrets from her.

"I was Bree's first date," he said softly.

Oh! He could have said anything. He could have

said he was a summer student who had worked for her father. But oh, no, he had to bring *that* up.

"I don't recall you being my *first* date," she said. "I'd had others before you." Freddy Michelson had bought her a box lunch at a fifth-grade auction. That counted. Why did he think he'd been her first date?

No doubt her well-meaning father had told Brand that his bookish, introverted daughter had not been asked to her senior prom. Or anywhere else for that matter.

She could have felt annoyed at her father spilling her secrets, but no, she felt, as she always did, that stab of loss and longing for the father who had always acted as if she was his princess, and had always tried to order a world for her befitting of that sentiment.

"Your first date?" Chelsea squealed, as if Bree had not just denied that claim.

Bree shot Brand a look. He grinned at her, unrepentant, the university student who had worked for her father during school breaks. The young man on whom she had developed such a bad crush.

She turned quickly to the fallen table, and tried to snap the fallen leg back up. It was obstinate in its refusal to click into place.

"Let me," Brand said.

"Must I?"

"You must," Chelsea said, but Bree struggled with the table leg a bit longer, just long enough to pinch her hand in the hinge mechanism. She was careful not to wince, shoving her hand quickly in her apron pocket.

"Here," he said, an order this time, not an offer. Bree gave in, and stepped back to watch him snap the leg into place with aggravating ease.

"Thanks," Bree said, hoping her voice was not laced with a bit of resentment. Of course, everything he touched just fell into place. Everything she touched? Not so much.

"Is your hand okay?"

Did he have to notice every little thing?

"Fine."

"Can I look?"

"No," Bree said.

"Yes," Chelsea breathed.

Bree gave Chelsea her very best if-looks-could-kill glare, but Chelsea remained too enamored with this unexpected turn of events to heed Bree's warning.

"Show him your hand," she insisted in an undertone.

To refuse now would just prolong the discomfort of the incident, so Bree held out her hand. "See? It's nothing."

He took it carefully, and she felt the jolt of his touch for the second time in as many minutes. He examined the pinch mark between her thumb and pointer, and for a stunning moment it felt as if he might lift her tiny wound to his lips.

She held her breath. Somewhere in the back of her mind she heard Chelsea's sigh of pure delight.

Of course, one of the most powerful men in Vancouver did not lift her hand to his lips. He let it go.

"Quite a welt," he said. "But I think you're going to live."

Feeling a sense of abject emptiness after he'd withdrawn his hand, Bree turned her attention to the boxes of cookies scattered all over the floor, and began to pick them up. He crouched beside her, picking them up, too.

"Please don't," she said.

"Thank you for your help," Chelsea said firmly, clearly coaching her boss how to behave around an extraordinary man.

"I can get them," Bree said.

But Brand stayed on the floor beside her, reading the labels out loud with deep amusement. His shoulder was nearly brushing hers. An intoxicating scent, like the forest after rain, tingled her nostrils.

"'Little Surprises,'" he said, reading the boxes. "'Love Bites. Devilishly Decadent. Spells Gone Wrong.' These are priceless," he said.

His appreciation seemed genuine, but she now felt the same about her cookie names as she had just felt about the apron and the beret. She felt *cute* rather than *clever*. She wished she had come up with an organic makeup line, like the woman at the booth set up across the foyer from her.

"Bree, are these your creations?"

"Yes, Kookies is my company."

"I like it all. The packaging. The names. I'm glad you ended up doing something unusual. I always wondered if it would come true."

The fact that he had wondered about her, at all, knocked down her defenses a bit.

She stared at him. "If what would come true?"

"That night, at your prom. Don't you remember?"

She remembered all kinds of things about that night. She remembered how his hand felt on her elbow, and how his same forest-fresh scent had enveloped her, and how every time he threw back his head and laughed her heart skipped a beat. She remembered dancing a slow dance with him. And she remembered that she, school bookworm and official geek, had been the envy of every other girl in the room. She remembered, when the evening had ended, leaning toward him, her lips puckered, her eyes closed, and him putting her away.

"Do I remember what?" she asked, her voice far more choked than she would have liked it to be!

"They gave out all those titles in a little mock ceremony partway through the dance. Most likely to succeed. Mostly likely to become prime minister. You don't remember that?"

"No."

"Most likely to become a rodeo clown, most likely to win the Golden Armpit for bad acting."

"Those weren't categories!"

"Just checking to make sure you were paying attention."

As if anyone would *not* pay attention to him. His grin widened, making him seem less *billionaire* and more *charming boy from her past.*

She remembered this about him, too—an ability to put people at ease. That night of the prom, gauche and starstruck, she had wondered if it was possible to die from pure nerves. He had teased her lightly, engaged her, made himself an easy person to be with.

Which was probably why she had screwed up the nerve to humiliate herself by offering him her lips at the end of the evening.

"Now that I've jarred your memory, do you remember what your title was?"

"I hardly remember anything about that night." This was not a lie. She remembered everything about *him*, but the other details of the night? Her dress and the snacks and the band and anyone else she had danced with had never really registered.

"Most likely to live happily ever after. That was the title they bestowed on you."

The worst possible thing happened. Not only was she here on the floor, picking up her mess with the most devastatingly attractive man she had ever met, in a silly apron, with her hair scraped back in a dumb bun and granny glasses perched on her nose, but now she was also going to disgrace herself by bursting into tears.

CHAPTER TWO

No!

Bree Evans was not going to cry in front of Brand Wallace. She had a broken dream or two, but so what? Who didn't?

She bit the inside of her cheek, hard. She made herself smile.

"Of course they did," she said. "Happily-Ever-After. Look. Here's the proof." She bought a moment away from the intense gaze of his eyes on her face. She picked through the boxes of cookies.

There they were, the favorite kooky cookie for when she supplied weddings. She opened a box and pulled a cookie from its wrapping.

Shortbread infused with strawberries and champagne.

She passed it to him, and he took a quizzical bite.

"There you go," Bree said, and hoped he could

not hear the tight, close-to-tears note in her voice. "Happily-Ever-After."

She watched as his eyes closed with pleasure. He was distracted, as she had hoped.

When he opened his eyes again, he smiled at her. "That is one of the oddest—and tastiest—combinations of flavors I've ever experienced. Ambrosia."

"Thank you. I'll tuck that away for a new cookie name."

But then she saw she might not have distracted him quite as completely as she hoped, because he was watching her way too closely. She felt as if his eyes locked on the faint quiver of her lip.

"My company has an event coming up, a charity ball in support of this same goal, to raise funds for the new wing of Children's. Do you think I could get you to supply some of these?"

Bree's mouth fell open.

"Of course," Chelsea said smoothly.

"I'm sure they will be planning some kind of midnight snack or party favor," Brand said. "Have you a card? I'll give it to my event planner, and she'll be in touch."

Being around him was a roller-coaster ride, Bree thought, as she turned, flustered, to get him her business card. For a stunning moment she had thought he was showing interest in her. He'd quickly doused that by saying his event planner would be in touch.

This kind of opportunity was exactly why she was at this event, Bree reminded herself firmly, turning with a bright, hopefully professional, smile to give him the card.

He slipped the card into his inside jacket pocket, and popped the rest of the cookie into his mouth. It drew her attention, unfortunately, to the rather sensuous curve of his lips as he chewed.

"Do you want to go for a quick coffee?" he asked her.

A roller-coaster ride!

The invitation seemed to take him by surprise as much as it did her.

"R-right now?" she stammered. "Things are just about to begin. See? People are going through to the auditorium. The program said Crystal Silvers is going to sing first."

"I don't care about that."

One of the most sought-after performers in the Western world, and he didn't care about that? He cared more about having coffee with her?

This was dangerous territory indeed.

Bree gestured helplessly at her display. "Oh, I couldn't possibly—"

"You're going for coffee," insisted Chelsea, who had never had a stubborn moment in her life—she was certainly changing things up tonight. Her tone was firm, brooking no argument.

"No." Bree aimed her best who-is-the-boss-here? look at her assistant.

Chelsea ignored it. "Go, I can handle this."

"No, I—"

"Go!" Chelsea said, and then, under her breath, she added, "Live dangerously, for Pete's sake."

"Unless your husband would object," Brand said smoothly.

Chelsea snorted in a most unflattering way.

Brand's gaze slid to Bree's ring finger. She

wanted to hide it behind her back as if its nakedness heralded some kind of failure.

"Boyfriend, then."

Chelsea rolled her eyes. "She doesn't have a boyfriend."

She was as oblivious to the daggered look Bree gave her as she had been to the who-is-the-boss-here? look.

"The last guy she met on e-Us was a loser."

Since Chelsea was so adept at ignoring Bree's looks, dancing happily with insubordination, Bree managed to step hard on her foot before she could elaborate on the e-Us thing. Chelsea gave her a sulky look, but clamped her mouth shut.

Even so, damage had been done. Bree could see him registering what e-Us was.

One thing that was obvious about someone like Brand Wallace? He'd never been on a site like e-Us in his life.

"We'll just go around the corner," he said persuasively. "Two old friends catching up."

"Old friends," Chelsea breathed. "Do *you* have, uh, a significant other, Mr. Wallace?"

"Does my dog count?"

Chelsea gave Bree a not-so-subtle nudge on her shoulder.

"I don't think—" Bree began.

"I'm interested in your business. You'll be back in half an hour," he assured Bree. "The first set will have hardly started. These things never go off quite on time."

Meaning he was very familiar with *these things*. Big surprise.

"I'll have you back before intermission."

"I bet he won't stick you with the bill, either," Chelsea said helpfully, sidling out of the way before Bree could get her foot again.

The firm line of his mouth registered disapproval as he registered that morsel of information about the sad state of Bree's dating life.

"Your young assistant looks more than capable of finishing the setup here." His voice was suave.

Chelsea preened. "More than capable," she said, and flipped her hair.

It would seem churlish to refuse. It would seem like she was *afraid* of him, and life and surprises and the very thing she tried to bake into all her cookies.

Magic.

It was that magical thinking that always got her in trouble, Bree reminded herself. He had mentioned business. She was not in a position to turn down this kind of connection to the business world.

"All right," she said, resigned. "A quick coffee."

Bree came face-to-face with her truth. She was terrified of believing in good things.

And terrified especially to believe in the happily-ever-after that men like him had made women like her yearn for since the beginning of time.

"For goodness sake," Chelsea said in an undertone, "lose the apron. And do something with your hair."

She ran a hand through it, and followed Brand, tilting her chin at him when he held the door open for her.

It was a beautiful spring evening in Vancouver, and Bree was aware her senses felt oddly heightened. The air smelled good from a recent rain, and plump crystal droplets fell from the blossom-laden branches of the ornamental cherry trees that lined the sidewalk.

There were two coffee places around the corner from the concert hall, and Bree liked it that Brand chose the independent shop, Perks, rather than the one that was part of a big chain.

It was cozy inside, with mismatched sofas and scarred old tables with brightly painted chairs clustered around them. It smelled heavenly, of coffee and exotic spices.

"Have you been here before?" he asked her.

"Just to introduce them to Kookies. They passed."

"Fools."

Brand said it with such genuine indignation. It was going to be hard to keep her defenses about her. But she had known that when she was trying to refuse his invitation.

"Thank you for saying so. But it wasn't personal. They already had a contract with someone."

"Humph."

She had managed to get rid of her apron, but remembered Chelsea's instruction to do something with her hair. "If you'll excuse me for just a sec, I'll go freshen up."

"What can I get you?"

She was going to say hot chocolate; coffee was out at this time of evening. But in the spirit of living dangerously and allowing life to astonish her, she didn't. "Surprise me," she said.

"Oh. That sounds fun."

Somehow, she was not at all sure he was talking about beverage selection! She excused herself hastily before he could see the blush moving up her neck.

She found the washroom, slipped inside and looked at herself in the mirror. What she saw was so ordinary as to be discouraging. Her light brown hair, average at the best of times, was pulled into a tight bun—even worse. She had gone very light on the makeup, so faint freckles stood out on her nose. She had on no lipstick, and she had worn glasses tonight instead of her contacts. A wholesome, old-fashioned look was exactly what she wanted when she was behind the table giving out cookie samples.

To have coffee with an old crush—who could coax a blush out of her with a turn of phrase—not so much!

She pulled her hair out of the bun. It fell, stick-straight, to her shoulders. She rummaged in her purse for a brush and added a touch of lip gloss.

It was an improvement, but she was aware she still felt very ordinary, the kind of workaday girl who was virtually invisible.

"Not in his league," she told herself. But then she saw the plus side of that: she could just relax. It was just old friends catching up, after all. Nothing would ever come of it, except maybe a beneficial business connection.

She went back out into the main room. He had chosen two love seats facing each other with a round coffee table in between. She walked over and sat opposite him.

"You've let your hair down," Brand said.

Physically, not figuratively, despite her intention to relax. She hoped he didn't think she had done it to impress him.

"More comfortable," she said.

"I always liked the color of your hair. It reminds me of sand on a sun-warmed beach."

He had remembered the color of her hair? She gawked at him. *Sand on a sun-warmed beach?*

Do not gawk at the celebrities, she ordered herself. *And do not take it personally*, she also ordered herself. It was obvious he knew his way around women. He had found her one redeeming feature and flattered her about it. And it had worked some terrible magic on her. She could feel her nerves humming so hard it felt as though her skin was vibrating.

"I always considered it mousy brown," she said.

"That is ridiculous."

If she wasn't careful, she was going to gawk again. Probably with her mouth hanging open.

Thankfully, the beverages were delivered. Two steaming cups were set in front of them. She took hers, blew on it gently so as not to blow a blob of foam right onto his forehead and took a sip.

"What is this?" she asked, delighted.

"So I did manage to surprise! You've never had it before?"

"No."

"It's a chai latte. Spiced sweet tea with steamed milk. You like?"

"Wonderful. I can taste the tea, which is so ordinary, but then the spices and the mound of sugar-crusted foam raise it to a new level."

Suddenly she wondered why he had picked it for her. And she found herself looking at *ordinary* in a different light.

"And what are you having?" she asked him.

"Coffee, black."

"Given the variety on the menu, that seems unadventurous."

"I save my adventuring for other arenas."

She was going to blush again! No, she was not. She would not give him the satisfaction.

"You have had some great adventures in business," she said, pleased that she did not miss a beat. "I've been reading about you, Brand," she said. "You've done so well."

"Ah, the *City* article. I had no idea that magazine was so widely read."

Bree doubted it had been before they featured him on the cover!

"I must say I didn't treasure anonymity nearly enough when I had it. Everyone suddenly knows who I am. It's a little disconcerting. But thank you. The success part seems to be luck and timing. I jumped on an opportunity."

"My dad loved the quote—'opportunity meets preparation.' He always thought very highly of you. He admired your work ethic. He was fond of saying, 'That young man is going places.'"

"He used to say the same thing to me. When not another person in the world was. I feel as if he was the first person who truly believed in me. That goes a long way in a young man's life, especially one with no father figure. I don't think I ever had a chance to tell him that. What his faith in me meant. I regret it, but I'm glad I've been given this opportunity to tell you."

It became evident to her this was why he'd invited her for coffee. It was an opportunity to tell her what her father had meant to him.

It was lovely.

So, why did she feel faintly resentful—as if she was a chai latte that had just been demoted to a very ordinary cup of Earl Gray?

He watched her now over the rim of his coffee cup. "I called several times after your dad died. I spoke to your mother. Did she tell you?"

"Yes, she said you had called and asked after me."

"One day I called and the number was out of service. I dropped by the house and it was empty. For sale, if I recall."

Bree took a sip of her drink, and let the spicy aroma fill her nostrils and warm the back of her throat before she replied. "I left for college. My mother felt lonely in the house, so she sold it quite quickly. Then she remarried and moved to San Francisco."

"Is she happy?"

"Yes, very." She did not say it seemed her mother had moved on to happiness with unseemly swiftness. Bree had felt so abandoned. Of course, there was nothing like feeling abandoned to leave a young woman looking for love in all the wrong places.

"What did you take? In college?"

Heartbreak 101.

"I took a culinary program. I'm afraid I didn't finish."

He cocked his head at her. "That doesn't seem like you, somehow."

She cocked her head back at him. "Doesn't it?" she asked, deliberately unforthcoming, and letting him know that really, he knew very little about her, past or present.

"In some ways, you are very changed," he told her.

For a moment, she felt panicked, as if the sad ending of the pregnancy that had forced her to leave school was written all over her. She hoped her face was schooled into calmness, and she made herself release her stranglehold on her mug.

He *still* made her nervous.

"Your confidence in high heels for one thing."

Relief swept through her at his amused reference to her clumsiness on the night of the prom. "Oh, geez, you must have had bruises on your arm the next day. I should have practiced. I clung onto you most of the night."

"And I thought you were just trying to feel my manly biceps."

Despite herself, she giggled.

"It was a really nice thing for you to do," she said. "To take the boss' dateless daughter to her senior prom. I don't think I thanked you. Of course, it didn't occur to me until later that it probably wasn't your idea."

"It wasn't," he confessed. "I didn't date girls like you."

"Girls like me?"

"Smart," he said. "Sweet."

Not quite as smart as anyone had thought.

"I bet you still don't," she said wryly.

"I'm more the superficial type."

He made her laugh. It was as simple as that.

"So," he said, leaning forward and looking at her intently, "tell me how you have passed the last years. For some reason, I would have pictured you the type who would be happily married by now. Two children. A golden-retriever puppy and an apple tree in the front yard."

Happily-ever-after.

She could feel that same emotion claw at her throat. It was exactly the life she had wanted, the dream that had made her so vulnerable.

He had her pegged. Well, you didn't rise as fast in the business world as he did without an ability to read people with some accuracy.

There was no sense denying it even if it was not in vogue.

"That is my type. Exactly," she said. She heard the catch in her voice, the pure wistfulness of it.

"It's what you come from, too. I can see that you would gravitate back to that. Your family was so…"

He hesitated, lost for words.

"Perfect," she said, finishing his thought.

"That's certainly how it seemed to me. Coming from one that was less than perfect, I looked at the decency of your dad and the way he treated you and your mom, and it did seem like an ideal world."

One she had tried to replicate way too soon after the passing of her father, with a kind of desperation to be loved like that again, to create that family unit.

It was only now, years after her miscarriage, that she was beginning to tiptoe back into the world of dating, looking again to the dream of happily-ever-after. So far, it had been a disaster.

"Are you, Bree? Happy?"

She hesitated a moment too long, and his brow furrowed at her.

"Tell me," he commanded.

Ridiculous that she would tell him about her happiness, or lack there of. He had worked for her father a long time ago, and somehow been persuaded to take the hopeless daughter to her prom. They were hardly friends. Barely acquaintances.

"Deliriously," she lied brightly. "My little company builds a bit each day. It's fun and it's rewarding."

"Hmmm," he said, a trifle skeptically. "Tell me, Bree, what do you do for fun?"

The question caught her off guard. She could feel herself fumbling for an answer. What could she say? Especially to someone like him, who moved in the sophisticated circles of wealth and power?

She couldn't very well say that she had all the Harry Potter books and reread them regularly, with her ancient cat, Oliver, leaving drool pools on her lap. That after Chelsea, seamstress extraordinaire, had showed her how, she had individually quilted each of the cookies on her aprons. That she was addicted to home-renovation shows, especially ones hosted by couples, who had everything, it seemed, that she had ever dreamed of. That she trolled Pinterest features about homes: welcome signs, and window boxes, and baby rooms.

It would sound pathetic.

Was it pathetic?

"My business takes an inordinate amount of

time," she said when her silence had become way too long.

"So you don't have fun?"

"Maybe I consider developing new cookie recipes fun!"

"Look, my business takes a lot of time, too. But I still make time for fun things."

Just then a man came over and squatted on the floor beside her. He stuck out his hand. "Miss Evans? I'm the manager here. Mr. Wallace leads me to understand you have a line of cookies. We'd love to try them. Have you got a minute?"

She looked over the manager's shoulder at Brand. He was smiling. He nodded encouragingly at her.

"Yes, I have a minute," she said. The manager got up and sat beside her. She started to tell him about Kookies.

When she looked over at Brand, he was gone. The love seat across from her was empty.

No goodbye.

But at least he hadn't stuck her with the bill.

Fifteen minutes later, she left Perks. They were going to give Kookies a trial term of six months.

She walked back to the concert hall. Outside the door, before going in, Bree debated only for a full five seconds before she pulled out Brand's business card with his phone number and called him.

"Hello?"

She had been expecting it to go to voice mail, since she thought he was probably now in the front row for the Crystal Silvers performance. But there was no background noise.

"I was expecting to leave a message," she said.

"Bree. What an unexpected pleasure."

"I was rehearsing my message!"

"Okay, just pretend this is my voice mail."

"All right. Hello, Brand. Thank you for a pleasant evening and for buying me coffee. I wanted you to know Perks is going to try my cookies for a trial period."

"Excellent!"

"Voice mail does not respond," she reminded him primly.

"Oh, yeah. Forgive me. Continue."

She took a deep breath. "Thank you, but you didn't have to use your influence for me."

"Of course I didn't *have* to. But what exactly would be the point of having influence if you didn't use it to help others?"

And then he was gone, no goodbye again. She contemplated the kind of man that would make a statement like that.

This was what her father had always seen: the decency of Brand Wallace, a guy who could be trusted to do the right thing, even with a starry-eyed eighteen-year-old girl, desperate to be kissed.

His innate decency made her feel shivery with longing. He appeared to be the polar opposite of Paul Weston, the college professor who had taken what was left of her heart after the death of her father and run it through the meat grinder.

But it would be a form of pure craziness to think that a woman like her could ever have a man like Brand Wallace.

On the other hand, who had ever looked at her hair before and seen sun-kissed sand?

She went in the doors, and could hear the music blasting out of the auditorium. Chelsea, looking a little worse for wear, was behind a completely rummaged-over sample table, dancing enthusiastically by herself to the loud music spilling out into the foyer. She danced salsa competitively and managed to look ultrasexy even in the cookie apron and beret.

She stopped when she saw Bree coming toward her. Sadly, it did not appear her sudden cessation of movement was because it had occurred to her it might be inappropriate that the table in front of her was badly in need of straightening.

"Did you have wine?" Chelsea demanded.

"No, I had a chai latte." Bree decided, then and there, she probably would never have one again. Those smoky, spicy exotic flavors would remind her of a surprisingly pleasant evening—and forbidden longings—for as long as she lived.

"Oh, you're all glowy."

Bree was pretty sure *glowy* was not a word, not that she wanted to argue the point.

"What has happened to the table?" Bree asked,

not wanting to encourage an interrogation from Chelsea. "It's a mess."

"Oh! About ten minutes before Crystal Silvers started to sing, the people just started to pour through the front door. They were on me like the barbarian hordes. Just grabbing things, ripping open boxes, uninvited. I have tidied, you know. There were wrappers all over the place. Anyway, somehow samples made it back to the lady herself. She sent out an assistant to tell me she loved our cookies, to expect a big order for her birthday blowout."

It was more than Bree had hoped for! So why did she feel curiously flat about it?

If that came through, along with the extra business from Perks, there would be no time for thinking about happily-ever-after, or lack thereof, as the case might be.

Thank goodness.

"Oh, there goes the glowy look," Chelsea said. "The frown line is back. Miss Worry rides again."

Bree deliberately relaxed her forehead. She hadn't even realized until tonight she was endangering her chances of aging gracefully because of her perpetual frown. Despite the fact she knew better than to encourage Chelsea, she could not stop herself from asking.

"What color would you say my hair was?"

Chelsea regarded Bree's hair, flummoxed, clearly thinking this was a trick question that she was not going to answer correctly.

"Brown?" she finally ventured.

Bree nodded sadly. "Just as I thought."

CHAPTER THREE

YOU DIDN'T HAVE to use your influence for me.

After Brand had disconnected the phone and put it back in his pocket, he made his way through the rain-glittered streets. He had decided to walk home. Going back to the gala after being with Bree Evans would have felt like getting dumped onto an eight-lane freeway after being on a quiet path through the country.

Despite her new proficiency with high heels, and the way she filled out her trim white blouse, she was still sweet and smart. Definitely adorable. Totally earnest.

And completely refreshing.

Those words—*you didn't have to use your influence for me*—just reinforced all those impressions of her.

Everybody wanted him to use his influence for

them. Even the manager at Perks had approached him, not the other way around. He'd recognized him from that blasted *City* article.

Brand came to his house, and stood back for a second, gazing at it through the walkway opening in the neatly trimmed hedge. His architect had called it colonial, a saltbox, and, thankfully, it was less ostentatious than most of the mansions on his street.

Inside, Beau, who seemed to be largely telepathic, had figured out he was home, and gave a deep woof of welcome.

When people asked why he'd gone with a single-family house instead of a superglamorous condo, he said he'd purchased the Shaughnessy heritage home because it was close to his office tower in downtown Vancouver, his golf course and the VanDusen Botanical Garden.

That seemed much easier than admitting he had purchased the house because he thought his dog would prefer having a tree-shaded backyard to a condo balcony.

He opened the front door he never locked. Anyone with the nerve to try and get by his one-hundred-and-thirty-pound bullmastiff deserved a chance to grab what they could before dying.

The dog nearly knocked him over with his enthusiastic greeting, and Brand went down on his knees and put his arms around him. They wrestled playfully for a few minutes, until Brand pushed away Beau, stood up and brushed off his clothes.

"You stink."

The dog sighed with pleasure.

"I met a woman tonight, Beau," he told the dog. "More terrifying than you."

Beau cocked his head at him, interested.

"And that was before she laughed."

Since the events of this evening were about the furthest thing from what he had expected when he'd headed out the door, it occurred to him that life was indeed full of little surprises. He had the renegade—and entirely uncomfortable—thought that maybe her cookies held predictions in them after all.

And he had eaten that one.

Happily-Ever-After.

But one lesson he had carried from his hardscrabble childhood, left far behind, was an important one.

Fairy tales belonged to other people. People like her.

Except, from the stricken look on her face when he'd asked her about her happily-ever-after, somehow her great ending had evaded her. Or she thought it had. She was way too young to have given up on a dream.

And it was none of his business why it had, or why she had given up hope on it, but he felt curiously invested—as if that night he had taken her to the prom, he had made a promise to her father, a man who had been so good to him, that he would look out for her.

Brand also felt, irrationally perhaps, that he had given Bree a dream he couldn't have and she had let him down.

She was, in many ways other than just the high heels, very different. All grown up, as he had noted earlier. Her hair had been very long, but now, once she had let it down, he'd noticed it was shoulder-length and very stylishly cut. She used makeup well, and it made her cheekbones stand out, high and fine. She hadn't had on lipstick when he'd first seen her, but when she had sat down across from him at the coffee shop, her lips had the faintest pink-tinged gloss on them, shining just enough to make a man's eyes linger there for a moment.

And yet her eyes, huge and brown with no makeup at all, were almost exactly, hauntingly, as he remembered them—owlish and earnest, behind spectacles.

Almost, because now there was a new layer there. Sorrow. For her father, of course, but maybe something deeper, too.

She had pegged it. He'd never dated a girl like her before her prom, and to be honest, never had again.

"And I'm not about to start now," he told the dog. He took off his jacket and threw it in a heap on the floor, then undid his shirt and took off his shoes and socks. He padded barefoot through his house.

The architect had kept the outer footprint of the house, as the historical society demanded, but the inside had been stripped to the bones and rebuilt in a way that honored the home's roots, yet still had a clean, modern aesthetic.

The kitchen was no exception. Except for the Elvis cookie jar in the center of a huge granite island, his kitchen was a modern mecca of stainless steel and white cabinets, photo-shoot ready.

The designer had convinced him to go with a commercial kitchen, both for resale value and for ease of catering large events at his home. So far, there had been no large events at his home. As good as it sounded on paper, he didn't like the idea of boisterous gatherings in *his* space. Home, for him, was a landing strip between business trips, one that was intensely private. It was what it had never been when he was growing up—a place of quiet and predictability.

The cookie jar was stuffed with Girl Guide cookies. Brand shared a fondness for them with his dog, but he wondered if his enjoyment was now compromised for all time after sampling Bree's wares. Not feeling ready to admit to that, Brand passed on the cookies, grabbed a beer from a fridge that could have stocked a cruise ship for a month and went to the media room.

The media room was bachelor heaven: deep reclining leather seats, set up theater style, and a wall-to-wall television set with surround sound. There were Elvis posters on every wall. He flopped into one of the chairs, while Beau took up guard in his dog bed at his feet. He turned on the TV set, and let the comforting rumble of sound fill the room. He flipped through to the hockey game that had been recorded in his absence.

"This is the life," he told Beau, a little too forcefully.

Beau moaned, and he was aware of an echo, as if this room, filled with everything any man could ever want, was empty.

Bree had done that, made him aware of emptiness, in one single encounter.

If there was one thing Brand was really good

at, in the business world and wherever else it mattered, it was heeding the subtle first tingles of a warning.

She was the kind of woman that would require more of a man.

No doubt most men would find her quite terrifying. That included him.

So, he knew what he had to do. Nothing. Absolutely nothing. Disengage. He'd already done way too much. In a moment of madness he'd actually given her his phone number. She had already shown she wasn't afraid to use it.

Or maybe she had been afraid, and used it anyway, which was much, much worse.

See? That's the kind of woman she was. Simple things could become complicated way too fast.

He thought of the new layer of sadness in her eyes. Was that from the death of her dad, or had something else happened to her? He thought of her trying to get that business off the ground by herself. He thought of her not having an answer about having fun. He thought of her assistant letting it slip that Bree was on a dating site, and was meeting losers who stiffed her with the bill. He thought about how good her father had been to him.

He took her business card out of his pocket. It was a well-done card. Glossy. Colorful. Professional. Memorable. Kookies for all occasions. Her number was already in his phone, because she had called him.

He took a deep breath, scrolled through to her information and added it to his contact information. He hesitated and pressed the green phone symbol.

She wouldn't answer. She was in the middle of—

"Hello?" Her voice was breathless.

He had the renegade thought he would like to make her breathless in quite a different way. It nearly made him end the call, because what the hell did a thought like that have to do with honoring her father by helping her out a bit? But there was no placing an anonymous call these days, so he sucked it up.

"Can't get the taste of your cookies out of my head," he said.

Funny that thinking about taste made a vision of her lips pop into his mind.

"I try to warn people," she said. "Spells and enchantment."

He thought of her lips again! That must be it. He was spellbound. Now would be a great time to tell her he had pocket-dialed.

"Aside from my charity function, I thought we should talk about the possibility of you supplying my office staff room. And meetings."

She was silent.

"Bree?"

"It's very kind, but—"

There was suddenly a great deal of noise.

"I'm sorry," she said, "it's intermission. I'm going to have to—"

"Meet with me next week."

"Um—"

Geez! He was offering her a huge opportunity here. What was the problem? While the rest of the world was yapping at his heels wanting things from him, she was resistant—the lone exception.

"I'll be in the office all day Wednesday," he said smoothly, "if you want to drop by and we'll figure out the details."

Again there was hesitation, and then she asked, "Around ten a.m.?"

"Perfect. My office is—"

"I know. It's in the article."

"The *damn* article," he said.

She rewarded him with that laugh, soft, like a brook gurgling over rocks. "Okay. Wednesday at ten. Dear Lord."

"What?"

"Crystal Silvers is walking toward me. Good grief. She hardly has any clothes on."

And then she was gone. Brand stared at his phone. "Beau?"

The dog lifted his head and gave him a watery-eyed look.

"You're an expert on all things stinky. I stink at relationships, right?"

The dog laid his head back down with a groan

as if there was no point in having bothered him with such a self-evident question.

"That's what I thought. I'm putting on my big-brother shirt."

He remembered the refreshing innocence about her. Crystal Silvers had been walking toward her, the chance of a lifetime, possibly, and she focused on the no-clothes-on part.

Innocent in a world that was fast. Old-fashioned in a world that could be slick. Real in a world that distracted with shock.

So, she needed a bit of coaching. His offer to get her under contract to supply his office was perfect. Of course, he could have left the details up to his office manager, but this way he would be able to check up on her a little bit, and make sure some great business opportunities came her way. And maybe, subtly, move her in the direction of happiness, which she so richly deserved.

"Not that I'm any expert on happily-ever-after," he muttered.

The dog wagged his stump of a tail in approval. One thing that both Brand and Beau knew was that Brand was not cut out for relationships. Brand's father had abandoned him and his mother. At six he had become the man of the family. He'd been there for his mom, and he still was, but he was pretty damn sure that his father's genetics ran strong through his blood.

"Ask Wendy," he said out loud.

The dog's tail stopped thumping, no doubt a coincidence, but still Beau and Wendy had never seen eye-to-eye. It had been okay when Brand was just seeing her, as he had been exclusively for two years.

But then, she'd moved in. You thought you knew a person until they took down your Elvis posters and replaced them with original works of abstract art. He'd had to rescue the cookie jar from the garbage. People as svelte as Wendy did not let cookies touch their lips.

Within twenty-four hours, she was planning a Christmas extravaganza. Here. In their home. In their private space. She thought they could easily host two hundred people!

Thankfully, in short order, Beau had chewed

through the sofa she had brought with her, a ridiculous antique thing that wasn't even comfortable. Next on the menu had been three pairs of her shoes, imported from Italy. For dessert, Beau had eaten her Gucci wallet, with her credit cards in it. All that had been left was three gooey strands of leather and one slimy half of her Gold card.

She had said, "It's the dog or me."

He'd paid for the wallet and shoes and sofa, and chosen the dog. But in his heart he knew it wasn't really about the dog. It was about being unsuitable for the kind of cozy domestic future she was envisioning. It had all been great when he could pick her up at her house, and take her out to dinner or a function, without her cosmetics and hair products all over his bathroom counter.

Something in him had already been itching to move on, three days after she'd moved in. He was pretty sure he would have got out of it, one way or another, way before the Christmas extravaganza, just as his father had done.

After Wendy's departure from his home and his life, Brand put the Elvis posters back up. The

Elvis memorabilia had been his mother's pride and joy. Her suite in the seniors home had not been able to accommodate even a fraction of her collection. Always emotionally fragile, she'd gone into hysterics trying to decide what she could keep and what she could part with.

Another reason for a rather large house in Shaughnessy.

Okay, it wasn't the most pragmatic reason to buy a house. But when he picked up his mother on Sunday afternoons and brought her to his home, she was so happy to see it. Somehow, having them around him, reminded him of exactly what he came from. And that might be the most important lesson not to forget.

As if on cue, his phone went off—it was the quacking ringtone he reserved for his mom, a private joke between them. He glanced at the clock. Late. He could feel himself tensing ever so slightly.

"Hi, Mom."

"There was a movie tonight," she told him. "*Abracadabra.* Have you seen it?"

"No, I heard it was good, though. Tell me about it." The tension left him as her happy voice described the movie.

It was, Bree told herself firmly as she glanced at her wavering image in the polished steel elevator cage that was whisking her up to the forty-third floor, a second chance to make a first impression. Technically, her third chance, if she counted the prom.

Even though she was going to pitch a cookie contract to Brand's office, there was no cookie beret today and no quilted apron.

Something in his voice when he had called her offering her the contract had given her pause. It was why she had hesitated. Did he consider her a charity that would benefit from his generosity? It was as if he had relegated her to a perpetual little-sister position in his life. No doubt he had done the same the night of the prom! No wonder he had refused her lips that night. Not that she was offering her lips today. Or even letting her mind wander in that direction.

No, today, Breanna Evans was erasing *cute* from his impression of her, erasing a cookie beret and a quilted apron. Today, she was going to be one-hundred-percent professional. Polished. Pure business.

And grown up!

Even the night of the gala, when he had pronounced her all grown up, it seemed to her now, in retrospect, it was something said to a thirteen-year-old that you had last seen when she was ten.

Toward this goal, Bree had dug deep into her resources and purchased a stunning deep red, bordering on burgundy, Chloë Angus hooded cloak to wear over her one and only business suit, a nondescript pantsuit in a color that might be best described as oatmeal. The cloak made her hair, piled up on top of her head in an ultrasophisticated look, seem like sun-kissed sand.

Then, to compound the insanity, she had bought a matching pair of heels. The shoes made her look quite a bit taller than she really was, and hopefully, more powerful, somehow, like a busy CEO. She wasn't quite as graceful in them as she wanted to be, but she wasn't planning on running a marathon wearing them, either—she just wanted to make a crucial impression.

The one to erase all other impressions.

"CEO," she muttered to herself in the elevator, and then more firmly said, "Chief executive officer. Who got a contract to provide Crystal Silvers with five thousand cookies for her birthday blow-out? You! That's who!"

She hoped the elevator didn't have security cameras that recorded sound. A security guard somewhere would be having a good laugh at her expense.

She was carrying two large, rectangular white bakery boxes of cookie samples, which she always took, as a gift, when she was pitching an office contract. Unfortunately, the samples would not fit into a briefcase. Or maybe that was fortunate: who knows what kind of money she would have spent on that power item?

The elevator stopped. Despite her pep talk to herself, her heart fell to the pointy toes of her new red shoes. She considered just riding back down. She felt overcome by nerves, despite all the money she had spent trying to shore up her confidence with the beautiful, subtle raven-imprinted cloak.

But when the doors whispered open on the penthouse floor of one of Vancouver's most exclusive downtown office towers, Bree took a deep breath and forced herself to be brave. The world did not reward cowardice after all!

She stepped out into a gorgeous foyer, and her feet sank into a deep carpet. Hard surfaces would have been so much better for the heels! The lighting was low, and she noted two white leather sofas facing each other. Beyond them was a receptionist desk, currently empty of a receptionist, in some kind of exotic wood. On the far wall, to the right of the elevator, a stone wall had water trickling down its face, and was embossed with shining, wet gold letters that announced she was at the right place, BSW Solutions.

It looked like a solid wall behind the receptionist's desk, but then a sliver of light appeared in it, and Bree realized there was a door hidden in the wall. It pushed open a little more, swinging out into the room.

And then it was flung back with such force that the door hit the wall. Bree took a startled step back just as a monster shot out the door and galloped toward her! Her surprised mind grappled with the fact it was a dog. Not just any dog, but the largest one she had ever seen. He was brindle-colored with a head the size of a pumpkin. He was dragging a leash, and slobber was flying from his mouth as he covered the distance between them in three gigantic bounds.

Was he going to jump on her? Her own safety was not as paramount in her mind as the new cloak and her cookies.

She let out a little shriek and took a step back. Her heel caught in the extravagant pile of the carpet, and she lost her footing and dropped the cookies. She windmilled her arms, trying to stay upright, but to no avail.

She fell on the floor and closed her eyes tightly, resigned to being killed by a beast in the luxurious foyer of Brand Wallace's business. Why did nothing ever go quite as she planned it?

After a full second of anticipating her imminent death, nothing happened.

She opened an eye and sat up. The beast had skidded to a stop, and as she watched he nudged open the lid of a box and began to gobble up three dozen or so Spells Gone Wrong cookies.

"Beau!" The tone commanded the dog's complete respect. He sat immediately at attention, eyes on his master, his cookie-encrusted muzzle the only evidence he had done anything untoward.

"Bree. Oh, my God, I'm so sorry."

Brand was standing over her, his forehead puckered with concern, his eyes on her face. He reached down to her and his hand, strong and warm, closed around hers. He pulled her up and then he just stared at her, as if he'd never seen her before. Somehow, he forgot to let go of her hand.

He was dressed casually, far more so than he had been the night of the gala. He was wearing a jacket over a T-shirt, faded jeans and a nice pair of leather loafers with tassels on them.

The stunned look on his face made the Chloë Angus cloak and the shoes worth every penny of the investment.

"Are you okay?" he growled.

"Yes, I think so. Just in a bit of shock. You don't expect, er, *that* in an office like this."

"No, I know. I apologize. It's unforgivable, really."

"Brand," she said firmly, "I could tell you a thing or two about unforgivable, and believe me—" she looked at the dog, comic in his contriteness "—he doesn't even register."

She was shocked she had said that, as if she was ready to share confidences from her sordid past with him, which she most certainly was not. His hand was still holding hers. That was the problem. She had just been attacked by a monster beast, but her hand in his made her feel safe and protected.

And about as far from a CEO as you could get!

"Are you sure you're all right?"

"Positive, though I do think we have to stop meeting like this."

He realized he was still holding her hand. He looked down at their joined hands with surprise, and then let go abruptly. He looked at his hand. He looked at her hair, and lifted his hand as if he was going to touch the scattered tendrils of what was left of her lovely upsweep. Then he looked at her cloak. It seemed as if he was debating whether or not he should be brushing her off, and then thought better of it. He jammed his hands in his pockets. Bree actually found herself smiling, and then chortling.

She could tell it took a lot to rattle Mr. Brand Wallace, but he was rattled now.

"This is not a laughing matter," he told her sternly, and then looked to the dog. "Bad dog."

The dog flinched at the reprimand, but then turned a repentant gaze to Bree. His stub of a tail thumped hopefully.

"It's okay," she told the dog. He came out of his seated position. His whole monstrous back end wiggled.

"It's not!" Brand said. The dog sat back down.

Just then a breathless girl came out the door that both the dog and Brand had come through.

"Mr. Wallace, I'm so sorry. He's never done that before! I was just bringing him in off the terrace, when he bolted. I just wasn't expecting it. One minute I had the leash, and the next I didn't."

Brand looked really annoyed, despite the explanation. "Jennifer, he knocked over our guest."

"No—no, he didn't," Bree said quickly. "He startled me and I took a step backward. I fell over all on my own."

The girl was close to tears. It was obvious she had a bad case of hero worship for her boss and felt far more terrible that she had let him down than that their guest had taken a spill in the main foyer.

"I'm so sorry," Jennifer said tremulously.

"I take the blame," Bree said, still smiling. She picked up the open, and now empty, box of cookies and held it up. Spells Gone Wrong was clearly written across the lid. "Things always go off the rails whenever I make them. When it's combined with Little Surprises, watch out!"

"Oh," Jennifer said knowingly. "Cookies."

"That dog could not have possibly smelled cookies through that door," Brand said. "It's impossible."

He looked hard at his young employee, and seemed to realize she needed forgiveness. Nothing could be changed now. Unfortunately, Bree's sense of him being somehow safe in a stormy world intensified when his tone softened as he addressed the girl.

"Cookies are his weakness. I'm afraid I give him the odd one. Keep a firmer hold on him next time, Jenn."

Jenn heard the *next time* and beamed. "He likes the vanilla Girl Guide cookies," she told Bree. "Mr. Wallace has a closet full of them for the days he brings Beau to work with him."

The girl's attitude reminded Bree so much of Chelsea being altogether too revealing about Bree's personal life that she laughed out loud. Brand—one of the most successful men in Vancouver's business community—owned the world's ugliest dog. And brought him to work with him. And fed him Girl Guide cookies.

"He probably won't eat Girl Guide cookies ever again now," Brand said woefully, looking at the empty box and the dog's cookie-encrusted muzzle.

"I'll take him, Mr. Wallace."

"No, it's okay, I've got him now. If you could look after this mess I'd appreciate it." He stooped and picked up the leash, though it was probably entirely unnecessary. The dog was stuck to him like glue, as he leaned into his leg.

The dog made a moaning noise, as the mashed cookies were packed up, and Bree looked at him. He gave her a woebegone look that she could not resist. She got down on one knee in front of him.

"Don't touch him," Brand warned, too late. "He stinks."

But she already had the dog's big, wrinkly face between her hands. "Did you call him Beau?"

"He mostly answers to 'bad dog,'" Brand offered, "but sometimes I call him Beau."

"Beau," she said softly. "You are not a bad dog. You have one of the most beautiful souls I've ever seen."

The dog regarded her thoughtfully, and then his big, ugly chops spread into an unmistakable grin. His big tongue whipped out and removed most of her makeup before she could move her face away. She laughed, and stood back up, while wiping at her face with a corner of her brand-new cloak.

She stopped, aware Brand was staring at her.

"What?" she said.

He was looking at her with the oddest look.

As if he had found a treasure he had waited his whole life to find. A woman lived for a look like that.

CHAPTER FOUR

BUT THEN HE spoiled it all when he said, "You look just like Little Red Riding Hood."

Just the look she was going for! Should she tell him he looked just like the Big Bad Wolf? Before she could, he spoke again.

"I've provided the wolf, I'm afraid. Beau usually doesn't like people."

Hmmm, he thought the dog was the wolf.

"Not that he's nasty or anything," Brand continued, "just colossally indifferent."

That look she thought she had seen was gone from his face and, in fact, Bree wondered if it wasn't her ever fertile imagination going into overdrive. She'd thought she had made a breakthrough in being perceived as an adult woman, but he was seeing a character out of a fairy tale!

"Let me show you around," Brand said, then

led her to the door and held it open for her. Beau sat as she passed.

"Look at him," Brand said, "anxious to prove he's the perfect gentleman, and *not* the Big Bad Wolf."

As she went by him, Bree had the impression that Brand was uncomfortable, as if he knew, in that split second, he had revealed something he didn't want to reveal, and was now covering his tracks as quickly as possible.

If his intention was to distract, the room she found herself in certainly did that!

It was like nothing she had ever seen before.

It was a huge open space, scattered with deep fabric chairs that could have been mistaken for boulders, if people were not sunk so deeply into them. A cat was curled up in one young lady's lap.

Bree shot Beau a look, but he was looking off into the distance, regally indifferent to the cat.

"The cat and him sorted things out a long time ago," Brand said. "He's terrified."

"People bring their pets to work?" she asked, astounded. It was one thing for the boss to bring his dog on occasion, but it was startling to see the cat.

Brand nodded. She noticed a colorful hammock was suspended by ropes from the arched wooden beams of the ceiling, and a bearded fellow swung gently, as he tossed a beanbag in the air above his head and caught it. At the far end of the room the whole wall was covered in the colorful footholds and handholds of a climbing wall. There was a ball pit, of all things, filled to overflowing with bright yellow and red and blue balls. Music, a flute she thought, flooded the area.

A guy walked by them in bare feet. "Hiya, boss. Beau."

The dog, as Brand had predicted, was indifferent to the greeting. Brand took her elbow and guided her through the rock chairs and past the hammock bed hanging in the middle of the room.

He ushered her into his office and dropped Beau's leash. The dog padded across the floor to a large doggie bed.

The office was beautiful and expansive. Floor-to-ceiling windows looked out over the cityscape, and beyond that she could see the ocean and mountains, still white-capped at this time of year. A gorgeous desk, possibly rosewood, with deep chairs in front of it, anchored the room, but off to one side two love seats faced each other over a glass-and-steel coffee table.

"This seems like the only conventional space on the whole floor," she said. "Except, of course, for Beau, who is, um, hardly conventional."

The dog did several circles on the bed, then with a happy sigh, laid down.

"What on earth is his breeding?" she asked. "I think the floor shook when he settled!"

"He's part bullmastiff. And part rhinoceros. I've held off on letting the world know there was a successful interspecies breeding. He's introverted. I don't think he could handle the attention."

"I can clearly see he's introverted," she laughed.

"I suspect you smell overwhelmingly of cookies. He really is introverted, as I said, largely indifferent to people, with the exception of me. Have a seat." He gestured to the love seats, rather than the seats in front of his desk. “Can I get you something?”

“No, thanks.” She sank into the masculine, distressed leather, and Brand took a seat on the identical one across from her. “Is that a Lalique?” she said of the vase on the coffee table between them.

“A leak?” he said, and looked around puzzled.

“The vase.”

Then she saw he was teasing her. His eyes sparkled with devilment.

“Yeah, their Midnight Blue collection. According to my designer, an investment.” He rolled his eyes.

She knew she should be entirely professional, and just get down to business, but as always, he had a gift for putting her at ease. Curiosity overwhelmed her. “Tell me about that space out there. I have never seen anything like it.”

“The thing about a business like mine is you can’t just go with one idea. You have to be looking for the next one, and the next one after that. You have to be continually evolving and you have to be light-years ahead of the competition and the copycats.

"I'm good at business," Brand said, "and maybe even great at it. But I'm not strong in creativity, and I don't have top-of-the-line tech skills. And so I want to attract the best and brightest computer and creative working minds in the business. And I want to keep them. I've researched what makes a happy and productive workplace, and it's evolving it. That guy in the hammock, tossing the beanbag? His name's Kevin. He had an idea that made the company ten million dollars last year. He is one guy I make sure to talk to every single day."

"That's a lot of cookies," she said with a gulp. "The article—correction, the damn article—never said how it all began."

She still felt nervous, and a little off balance. But, of course, here she sat, Little Red Riding Hood, hair in shambles, her makeup licked off and her cloak askew. It would be good if she could get him talking until her wits came back!

"I had an idea a few years back—kind of Uber

meets Facebook, only in real time. I was traveling overseas for the company I worked for at the time. I was in Copenhagen and had a couple of hours on my hands. I thought, I wonder if I could find a pick-up game of hockey anywhere?"

She couldn't help herself. She laughed.

"What's so funny?"

"It's just so Canadian. And so *guy* somehow."

He smiled. That smile! So charming. So sexy! He leaned forward. His gift, or one of his gifts, was that he could make anyone feel as if they were the only person in the world that mattered to him.

"I know. A more sophisticated guy probably would have been checking out the museums and art galleries and restaurants. But I'd been on airplanes and in meetings for three days and I just wanted to blow off some steam and get very physical."

She felt her admiration for him grow even more. Because, really? If a guy like him wanted to get physical… She had to wrestle the blush that was threatening back down her throat.

Instead, her tone completely professional, she said, "It seems ironic that this hugely successful company came out of a desire to play hockey."

"I know, there is a bit of a bizarre element to it. Even more so because I was in no way unhappy with what I was doing. Loved my company. Loved the job. But this idea wouldn't let me go."

She actually had a general idea, from the magazine article, exactly where his thought of playing hockey in Denmark had taken him, but she was enjoying hearing about the birth of his company from him, directly and in detail.

"Intents was born. I liked how the name said one thing, but if you said it out loud it sounded like another—intense.

"The premise is you find yourself in a strange city, or country, but you like playing hockey or you like rock climbing or you like going to the opera or you like playing chess. An app shows you where to find those activities, and also people nearby who might be available to do them with you. You've been security-checked, they've been security-checked. It's all totally free. The pop-up ads on the website and app pay for it."

"It's quite brilliant," she said.

"Thanks, I'm proud of it. One of the things that surprised me, but is very satisfying, is how deep, lasting friendships come out of these connections sometimes. It's simply a great way to meet people who like the same things as you. We've had several weddings as a result."

"That isn't a dig at me meeting a guy on e-Us is it?"

"Who stiffed you with the bill," he reminded her.

"Thank you, Chelsea," she said. They both laughed, but when the laughter died, he was looking at her intently.

"What did you mean when you said you could tell me a thing or two about unforgivable?" he asked softly.

"Wh-what?" she stammered.

"When I said the dog knocking you over was unforgivable, you said—"

"I know what I said. A slip." She was *not* telling him. She clamped her mouth firmly shut and folded her arms over her chest. "Let's talk about cookies," she said brightly.

"I don't think you should be meeting people on e-Us," he said.

"Really?" she said. He did not appear to hear the coolness in her tone. "That's the accepted way of meeting people in this day and age."

"Well, it sucks."

She thought back over the majority of her experiences on e-Us. He had her there. "How would you suggest meeting people?"

"You like books? Go to a bookstore and tap some guy on the shoulder. Ask him what he's reading."

"That seems very forward. And maybe even dangerous."

"Unless he's in the memoirs-of-serial-killers section, you're probably okay," he said drily. "Geez, meeting a complete stranger, whose profile you've seen on the internet, is better somehow?"

"It's always in a public place. For a cup of coffee. Not very different than what we did the other night."

"I am not a complete stranger! I'm sure you knew, from our former acquaintance, I wasn't going to wait outside in the parking lot and club you over the head. Or follow you home. And I'm sure you knew I wasn't going to stiff you with the bill."

"Thank you, again, Chelsea."

"Not that I've been on one of them—"

She'd guessed right on that account!

"But it seems to me the problem with dating sites would be you can't get a read for people, the way you do when you meet them in person. The site is filtering all the facts. Even the picture can be a lie, can't it?"

She would certainly not admit that her last date had looked at least ten years older than he had in his profile picture.

"Plus there's the problem of sitting across from someone you barely know in a coffee shop. How does that not end up feeling awkward? Like an interview?"

She hated it that he, who had never been on a

dating site, was picking up the weaknesses of the system.

Why was it that this meeting, which was supposed to be an interview of sorts, did not feel like one at all?

"If you'd seen that guy in the bookstore, your little hinky sense would have told you—jerk. Something about the way he was standing, or the hole in his jeans, or the kind of book he was reading."

"Especially if he was in the serial-killer section!"

"More subtle. *How to Get Your Internet for Free, Collecting Coupons for Dummies.*"

She had the awful thought this was why she was really here. Despite her every effort to be the consummate professional, to correct those first impressions, here they were again.

With him feeling some kind of obligation to take care of her!

She had to get this back on track. The encounter with the dog had literally knocked down her defenses!

"All right," she said brightly. "I'll get the Intents app on my phone. Next time I'm in Denmark, I'll meet some fellow Harry Potter fans. I'll probably end up marrying one."

Harry Potter? Had she really said Harry Potter? She, who wanted to appear so grown up?

"Is that guy on the hammock out there single?" she said in a rush to correct impressions. "Maybe, on my way out, I'll just stop and ask him what he's throwing around. Is he single?"

"He is," Brand said drily, "but you have to speak Klingon to interest him."

"Klingon," she repeated, playing along. "I could learn. How often would I have to watch *Star Wars* to pick it up?"

"*Star Trek.* A mistake I'm okay with. Kevin? Not so much."

He was smiling. As if he found her intensely amusing! And here she was playing along with him. Well, enough was enough!

"Is that why I'm really here? Not to sell you cookies, but so that you can give me unsolicited advice about my personal life?"

CHAPTER FIVE

BREE KNEW SHE should stop right there, but she didn't.

"Despite playing the role at my senior prom, you are not my big brother!"

"You're right," Brand said. "I'm sorry. I've overstepped. I was acting like your protector, and—"

So, she *had* guessed right. She was here out of some form of sympathy. Support for the old boss' daughter. Okay, just the tiniest bit of weakness unfolded in her when he said *protector* like that. Oh! To have a protector such as him! She felt as if she had been on her own, with no one to lean on, for so long.

But, no! She was not giving in to that weakness. She was here to correct that very impression. That somehow she needed something that only he could give her.

She knew she was never going to be able to dislodge that first impression, not even if she went out and bought four hundred Chloë Angus capes. It was set in his mind. He was always going to see her as a hopelessly naive young girl. Nothing she had done today, from tripping over carpets to kissing dogs, had corrected that impression. Even the fact that she was sophisticated enough to recognize a Lalique had gone completely over his head!

Brand Wallace was buying her cookies, entering a business arrangement with her, out of pity! Out of some misguided desire to help her.

Suddenly she knew one way to correct his impression of her. To make him realize he didn't know her at all. The boldness it required stole her breath. It made her realize maybe her impressions of *herself* also needed a bit of tweaking.

She got up. She felt like a soldier going into battle. Her heart was beating so hard that surely he could see it hammering, right beneath the cloak. Some sort of momentum carried her across to his sofa. A granite determination overtook her as she sank into the seat beside him.

She could hear the frantic roar of her own heart in her ears.

She leaned closer to him, put both hands on either side of his face and drew him to her. Her heart went still. A great and surprising calm overtook her.

His cheeks, beneath her fingertips, were ever so slightly whisker-roughened, as if she was touching sandpaper. His scent was pine and rain and man. His eyes were the deepest brown she had ever seen, and the devilment in them had been replaced by surprise. And understandable wariness.

He was a man not accustomed to being caught off balance, and she had put him off balance. He was a man accustomed to calling the shots, and right now, in this surprising instant, she was calling the shots.

If she dared.

She saw it in his eyes that he knew what was coming, but was not sure she had the nerve.

She hesitated for one moment at the edge of the

cliff, terrified of the dizzying height she stood at. And then she jumped.

And felt the exquisite and glorious freedom of freefall. She kissed him. She kissed him hard, and she kissed him passionately. She kissed him until neither of them could breathe. She kissed him until any resistance from him melted and his hands were tangled in her hair and he was kissing her back, his delicious lips nuzzling her own, exploring her own, claiming her as his own.

She lost the point of the exercise. Somewhere, she lost herself. Her world became so small, only this: his lips, the taste of them and the texture of them and the suppleness of them and the force of them. Her world became so large, only this: the stars in the sky, and the birds in the trees and the rivers flowing endlessly to the sea. All the mysteries were in this one small thing.

It seemed it might go on forever. There was that word, *forever*, that beautiful, enticing, enigmatic word from fairy tales.

But then the whole love seat seemed to groan, and his lips left hers.

"Beau!"

The dog had hefted himself up on the couch, and inserted his bulk gingerly between them. His huge tongue was flattened across the whole of Brand's cheek, slurping upward in slow motion.

With an impatient shove, he put the dog off the couch and wiped at his soggy cheek with the sleeve of his jacket.

Before she could lean back in and offer her lips again, Brand leaped off the love seat. He stared down at her. He ran a hand through his hair. He paced away from her.

"Harry Potter fans of the world, beware," he muttered. "What the hell was that about?"

Bree made herself sit up straight. She took a deep breath. She adjusted her cloak. She touched her hair. Her upsweep was now totally unswept.

Still, she made her voice firm. "I am not some cute child who has showed up at your office selling cookies, like a Girl Guide going door-to-door," she said.

"Okay, I think you've made that point."

"And I am not the gauche girl who was so innocent you could not risk a kiss good-night after her senior prom."

He swore under his breath. He was looking at her way too closely. "Have you been nursing that little grievance all these years?"

"No!"

"I think you're lying," he said softly.

"Well, you don't know anything about me."

He touched his lips. "That's true," he conceded.

Suddenly, she was mortified. She had just kissed Brand Wallace! What would he think she *was* selling? She thought of apologizing, and then she thought better of it.

Okay, it might not have been the most professional thing she had ever done, but really? From the look on his face, he was never going to think of her as a child again!

And really? She felt alive, and powerful. She felt she was practically sizzling with energy and life and passion.

"Now," she said, "are we ready to talk business?"

Under his breath, he said something that sounded

like a word a sailor might say. He looked downright wary. That was better!

"I'm not sure we're done discussing *that*."

"We are," she said firmly.

"If you didn't think of it for six years, where did that come from?"

"It's Spells Gone Wrong," she said, lifting a shoulder. "Again. Deadly, in combination with Little Surprises."

"You must have brought some Devilishly Decadent, too," Brand said drily.

He remembered the names of her cookies! *Stay on track*, Bree ordered herself.

"You're right, I must swear off delivering that particular combination of cookies. And speaking of cookies, how many people are in your office? I usually recommend starting with two cookies per person per day. Initially, I'll send quite a variety, but I'll give you a voting sheet to put on the coffee table. Then I'll start sending what people like best. If I was going to guess for this office? Earth Muffin. Vegan cookies..."

* * *

Brand watched Bree. She seemed composed enough after what happened, but if he was going to guess? She probably didn't usually talk this much.

Still, as she detailed her ordering and billing procedures, he noticed that, despite the rather shocking interchange that had just occurred between them, she had a really good business head on her shoulders. Nothing *kooky* about that part of her.

This whole fiasco was his own fault.

He'd been rattled since the first moment when he'd found her on the floor. His sense of not being in control had deepened when he had seen how she had reacted to the dog licking off her makeup.

No shrieking. No hysterics.

And she hadn't been putting it on to impress him, either. She genuinely loved animals.

But nobody loved Beau!

Except him.

This suddenly felt like one of the scariest moments of his life: she looked like Little Red Riding Hood, and kissed like a house on fire. She wove spells into her cookies. And she could see the souls of dogs.

He had known she was going to kiss him. He'd known it as soon as she sank down on the couch beside him.

He'd known and yet, he had not moved. He'd been caught in some spell of curiosity and enchantment.

He had to get her out of here, and out of his life. She was right. Absolutely right. She was totally grown up. One-hundred-percent pure woman. She'd proven that beyond a shadow of a doubt. There was nothing brotherly about the way he was feeling about her.

"Okay," he said abruptly. "Where do I sign?"

"I'll email you a contract with the terms we've just discussed."

City magazine would love to see him now. The man they'd declared to be the businessman of the decade was going to be emailed a contract and he had not the slightest idea what was in it, or what they had just discussed.

He forced himself to focus on her. A mistake. Her hair was scattered around her face. She was glowing. Her lips looked faintly bruised. She looked more like a woman who had just had some loving laid on her than one who had just made a great sale.

“Cookie delivery will start on Monday,” Bree said, a complete professional *now*. “The cookies have a shelf life, not refrigerated, of six days. I like to leave them only for a maximum of three. My delivery guy will change out any older cookies when he comes midweek. We donate them to a kitchen that feeds the homeless. Is that okay with you?”

“Fine,” he said.

She stood up. “Thank you for your business, Brand.” For a moment, her in-charge businesswoman persona faded. She took her hand out of her cloak, looked at it and looked at him as if she was considering offering it.

He could feel himself holding his breath. He really did not want to risk the temptation touching her again would no doubt create!

Thankfully, she saw his hesitation, tucked her hand back under her cloak and went out the door. He was aware, as it whispered shut behind her, that he was exceedingly tense.

He deliberately rolled back his shoulders, shrugged them up to his ears, then let them slide back down. He shot his dog a dirty look.

"Traitor."

Beau opened one eye and thumped his tail a few times. If he could talk Brand was pretty sure he'd say, "Look, buddy, we both kissed her. How is it I'm the traitor?"

"What did I just order, anyway?"

Bree rode the elevator down. "CEO of the century!" she told her reflection. Despite things going slightly off the rails—well, a lot off the rails if it came to that—it was a great contract.

She was not going to think about that kiss! Or the taste of him. Or the way he had looked after she had kissed him. Baffled and off-kilter and aware of her in a whole new way!

She was not going to think about what strange

madness had overtaken her. She suspected he was right.

It was comeuppance for his rejection of her lips all those years ago. She probably had thought of it way more than she should have. Well, now she knew. She knew what he tasted like. She knew she could make him see her as a woman, not a child. She knew and she could put that all behind her.

She was not thinking of that anymore. He could be the worst possible kind of distraction. She was going to keep him at arm's length. She didn't have to see him again, and she was not going to indulge the little swoop of loss she felt right in her tummy at the thought of not seeing him again.

She was thinking of her business. How could she be in close proximity to those lips and still think about her business? So, proximity was out.

Between this, the new Perks contract and her special order for Crystal Silvers, Kookies for All Occasions was in the best shape it had been in since she had started the company.

Her phone vibrated in her pocket just as she exited the office building.

It was Chelsea, and she was talking loudly and rapidly, on the verge of hysteria. Bree had to hold her phone away from her ear.

"Chelsea, slow down. What happened?"

The story came out, bit by disjointed bit. When Bree understood completely, she froze in shock. But this is what she should have remembered about life: for her, good things were followed by disaster.

Since her father had died, it seemed that lesson got hammered home again and again. She had fallen in love with Paul, head-over-heels in love, shamelessly blinded by what she had felt for him. It had been, she thought, the best thing that ever happened to her.

The pregnancy had shown her his true colors. She had been shocked by how, underneath all that charm, he was self-centered and mean-spirited. He had accused her of doing it on purpose! Paul had seemed like the most romantic of men, but it had really been nothing more than manipulation of a vulnerable, very young and hopelessly naive woman. His abandonment had been complete and immediate.

That's what she knew about unforgivable!

Still, there had been the pregnancy, acting as a beautiful buffer to complete heartbreak. Of course she had been afraid. Of course her life had been disrupted. But underneath all that had been a little hum of joy that walked with her, a constant, through her days.

A baby. Her baby, growing beneath her heart. She sang it lullabies of pure love. She talked to it of hopes and fears.

But her joy stopped abruptly with the miscarriage, and never, if she thought about it, ever really came back. Not completely.

"I am not thinking about that right now!" she said fiercely, out loud, not caring who sent wary glances her way.

No, she was not going to pathetically catalog her heartbreaks and disappointments because of the blow Chelsea had just delivered.

She was harnessing the energy of her visit with

Brand. The aliveness of it. The powerful surging energy, a sense of not being able to do anything wrong.

"I am the CEO of the century," Bree reminded herself. "I've been given a problem. A big one, but there is no point in crying over spilt milk. I need to find a solution, not fold up my tent and creep into the night!"

But forty-eight hours later, exhausted and broken, she admitted defeat.

With what was left of her strength she called his number. For some reason, it felt as if it was going to be her hardest call and so she made it first.

"Bree! I've been waiting for that contract."

She had steeled herself to sound only business-like. Did he have to sound so happy to hear from her?

"I'm sorry."

"Bree?"

"There isn't going to be a contract."

"Are you crying?"

"No."

"Not because of what happened here, I hope."

"I am not crying." But she was. Still, he couldn't see her, red-faced and snotty-nosed, the antithesis of the woman she had been two days ago.

So, he was still thinking of that kiss. Well, so was she. The taste of his lips—and the surprising boldness that she was capable of—was one of the few things that had sustained her through forty-eight hours of hell.

"*If* I was crying it would have nothing to do with what happened there."

"What's wrong?"

She found herself unable to speak.

"You *are* crying, aren't you? Where are you?" he asked.

"I'm at my apartment."

"I'm coming over."

"No, I—"

"Give me the address."

Oh, the temptation. There it was again, that foolish weakness, not wanting to be so alone with it all. To just lean on someone else, even for a little while.

"There's been a…situation, and I need to shut the company down temporarily." She had planned to tell him she hoped perhaps she would be up and running again in a few months, but she knew she could not keep control, so she quickly ended the call. "Goodbye, Brand. It was nice connecting with you again. Thank you for the opportunity."

"Bree—"

She disconnected.

She looked at herself. Of course he couldn't come over. Her whole apartment was smaller than his office. It was three o'clock in the afternoon and she was still in her pajamas. Her hair was tied up on top of her head with a neon orange shoe-lace. Her eyes were puffy. She wandered into the kitchen and opened the fridge. There was nothing in it. Well, a bottle of unopened wine, left over from a girls' night several weeks ago.

She could not have a drink. That was no way to deal with sorrow. It would be the beginning of the end.

Defiant of the bleak future the wine promised, she took the bottle out of the fridge. It wasn't even good wine. An Australian screw-top. If she ordered a pizza, it would be okay to have a glass. Lots of people—grown-ups—had a glass of wine with their pizza.

It might be a good idea to eat something, come to think of it. Chocolate ice cream and the broken cookies she'd brought home could not sustain her forever. Plus, she was out of the ice-cream part of the equation. She called for a pizza, and took the wine into her tiny living room. Her cat, Oliver, was in her favorite chair, so she took the less comfortable couch.

She poured a glass of wine and eyed it. Red. She didn't even like red wine. It generally gave her a headache. She closed her eyes without sampling the wine.

The doorbell rang. Had she fallen asleep? She glanced at the clock. Only a few minutes had passed.

The pizza place was just down the street, but that was fast, even for them. She looked at her disheveled state: Oliver-approved pajamas with cats on them, furry slippers that looked like monster feet, her hair uncombed, her face unwashed.

She didn't owe an explanation to the pizza-delivery boy! He probably saw it all. Wasn't there even a commercial about that? Where a guy goes to the door in his underwear to get his pizza? Still, she found herself formulating a story about the flu as she opened the door.

The shock was so great, she tried to close it again.

CHAPTER SIX

"GET YOUR FOOT out of my door," Bree said. She shoved hard on the door. She felt like a mouse trying to move a mule.

"No."

"What are you doing here? I never gave you my address." Having failed to shut the door, she tucked herself behind it and peeked out at him. This was worse than being seen in her Kookies apron and beret. She was an absolute mess.

He, of course, was not. A mess. Or anything close to it. He was supremely put together in a light blue button-down shirt, dark chinos, boots, a black leather jacket and a scarf. She thought one man in a thousand could wear a scarf well. Naturally, he would be that one.

"I work with the world's best computer geeks," Brand said smoothly. "Your address, to them?

Child's play. A great big yawn. Not even a challenge. Had it in my hand forty seconds after I asked for it."

"I'm not sure if that is completely ethical," she said crisply, from her station behind the door.

He cocked his head at her. "I'm not sure it is, either," he said thoughtfully. "But you should think of how easy it was next time you are arranging to meet a stranger on e-Us."

"How did you get in the front door of the building?"

He blinked at her twice, slowly, demonstrating his hypnotic charm. "This is a face that inspires trust, particularly in a little old lady trying to manage an unruly beagle and a bag of groceries at the same time."

"Mrs. Murphy," she said, annoyed. "Why are you here, Brand?"

And why did he have to look so good? Strong, and put-together, and sure of himself, the kind of guy a woman in a weakened state might want to throw herself at.

"I wanted to make sure you were okay."

"Well," she said, "you can clearly see I'm okay."

"You're hiding behind a door. How do I know if you're okay? Maybe one of your computer dates hit you over the head with a club."

She stepped out from behind the door. "See?"

He looked her up and down. He looked insultingly unconvinced about her okayness. He stared at her feet for a long time before he looked up again.

"You look as if you've been crying," he said softly.

"I have the flu, sick to my stomach, cold symptoms, runny nose, puffy eyes. You know," she said, relieved she had prepared an excuse for the pizza-delivery boy.

Who chose that minute to get off the elevator, in his distinctive red ball cap and shirt, and come to her apartment door.

"Your front-door security clearly sucks," Brand noted in an undertone.

"Medium, everything on it, double anchovies?" the delivery boy asked cheerfully.

Brand raised an eyebrow at her. "Flu food?"

She glared at him and turned to get her wallet out of her pint-size kitchen. When she returned the pizza boy was gone, and Brand was inside, holding the box, her door shut firmly behind him.

"Really? Double anchovy?" he asked.

"My weakness."

"Mine, too."

She searched his face for the lie and found none.

"Can we share it?" he asked. He was grinning that boyish grin, the same one that had, no doubt, sucked Mrs. Murphy into letting him into the building. Bree found herself as helpless as Mrs. Murphy. Who on earth could resist this overpowering charm?

"Since you paid for it, would it seem churlish to refuse?"

"Yes."

"You didn't have to come."

"No, I didn't. What can I say? I find a damsel in distress irresistible."

Somehow, with Brand, there was no point telling him he did not have to do the decent thing.

"I seriously doubt there is one thing about me

that is irresistible at the moment," she said as she led him through to the tiny living room. Oliver gave him a disdainful look and curled into a tighter ball, which left them the option of sharing a too-small couch. Brand sat down on it.

"I should go get dressed. I'm at my worst."

"Well, I've already seen it, so I wouldn't get too twisted. It's not as if I can unsee it."

She flopped down on the couch beside him. "The old 'no point shutting the barn door after the horse is out,' eh? That bad?"

He slid her a look. "Kind of adorable."

"Adorable," she said glumly. He was ready for his *GQ* cover and she was adorable. "Like a Pomeranian puppy?"

"More like a Yorkie. It's the furry-feet slippers. And the bow in your hair. You know how Yorkies wear those little bows on their heads?"

She reached up and yanked the shoelace out of her hair.

He sighed. "The adorable factor just went down, oh, maybe five points."

Don't indulge him, she ordered herself. "On what scale?"

"Out of a hundred. Being a perfect hundred before and now minus the five points."

"If I take off the pajamas?"

He went very still.

"I didn't mean it like that." She gave him a good hard punch in the arm.

He held his arm and made a face of exaggerated pain. "Oh. Okay. I just couldn't be sure. Because of that kiss—"

She punched him again. "Don't ever mention that to me again!"

"Bossy. Another five points off. And ten for each time you hit me in the arm."

"I should be a rottweiler pretty soon then. I can only hope. People respect rottweilers," she muttered, though inwardly she was greatly enjoying his banter. Only because it was proving a distraction from the last few days, which had been so without lightness of any kind.

"You have the feet for a rottweiler," he suggested.

She kicked off the slippers.

"Minus two for losing the slippers. Cute feet, though. Are your toenails lime-green? Plus twenty."

"With flowers." She held one up for him to inspect.

"Impressive. Plus twenty-five."

"It's not really my style, but Chelsea wants to work in a spa someday, once she gives up salsa dancing. Her toes are always showing for competitions, so she's very good at nail polishes. Still, she likes to practice on other people, namely me. I don't let her touch my fingernails, though, just the parts of me that usually don't show!"

He eyed the glass of wine, the bottle beside it. "For someone a little inhibited it seems like it might be a bit early for that," he said.

"Too early for anchovies?" She grabbed her wineglass. She took a defiant sip. Inhibited? Who had kissed whom?

"You better tell me what's going on." His shoulder was touching hers. Warmth radiated through his jacket. The leather was soft and supple, and if expense had a smell, the scent coming off the jacket would be it. Brand put the pizza box on the hassock and opened it.

She set down her wine and took the piece of pizza he offered. There was no way to eat an everything-on-it with any kind of decorum, but it was too late to make a good impression now, anyway. She was suddenly starving.

Come to think of it, she was all done making impressions. She took a huge bite of the pizza and chewing it gave her a few moments to put her thoughts together.

"You can see from the size of this place, I wasn't making cookies here." She kept her voice firm. "I rented space in a commercial kitchen. It burned to the ground two days ago, just as I was leaving your office, actually. Chelsea was there. I don't want to say Chelsea burned it to the ground, but she does get distracted practicing her routines while the cookies bake. There's some talk of a lawsuit. The building owner advised me to retain a lawyer."

"Ouch."

“Do you know what that costs?”

“Unfortunately.”

“If that wasn’t bad enough, I lost all my stock and some of my equipment and inventory. Insurance will cover some of the stock and inventory—unless Chelsea is found liable. Then I would have to sue her personally, which I don’t think I could do, under any circumstances, even if she was practicing salsa dancing and got distracted and caught the kitchen on fire. She’s so upset already.”

“Do you have another wineglass?”

“Kitchen cupboard beside the range.”

He got up and she watched him go. His shoulders practically touched either side of the galley-kitchen door frame. Her place was small, and now it seemed smaller, as if he was filling it—not just the floor space, but the air. He would leave, but still be here. She would breathe him in forever. She might have to move. On top of everything else.

She sighed heavily. Brand came back with a coffee mug instead of a wineglass. He poured himself some wine. He sampled it cautiously. "Not as bad as I thought it would be."

"My story?"

"No, that's worse than I thought it would be. The wine's pretty good, though I'm just drinking this to keep you from downing the whole bottle yourself. Not that you don't have reason, but I don't want to see you get drunk. Lose your inhibitions—"

She cocked her fist at him.

"I wasn't going to mention the thing that must not be mentioned." His eyes went to her lips, and stayed there for a heated second until he looked away.

Had he deliberately paraphrased a very famous line from a series of books she had admitted, in an unguarded moment, to liking? Did that mean he had read them?

Possibly just seen the movies, which was way more resistible.

"A gentleman until the end," she said wryly.

"I try," he said.

"This is one of those surreal moments," she decided. “Here I am in my hobbit-sized apartment with a view of the side of the building next door, serving cheap wine in a coffee mug to the man being lauded by *City* magazine as the billionaire businessman of the decade.”

“Don’t forget the furry-feet slippers and the shoelace,” he said, beautifully unimpressed with himself.

“This could only happen to me.”

“You’re probably right. Cheers.”

“Cheers,” she said. They rapped their glasses together.

“I like your hobbit-sized place,” he said. “It’s homey.”

“Humble.”

“Don’t worry about it, Bree. I’m not really a gentleman.”

“What? Of course you are!”

He wagged his eyebrows fiendishly at her, but there was something in his voice when he spoke again. “I’m just a pretender at the genteel life. What I come from makes this place look like a palace.”

"Really?" But then she remembered something he had said the night of the gala. He had said her family looked perfect, particularly to someone who came from one that was not. He had mentioned he had no father figure.

He nodded.

Suddenly, she *needed* to know. She needed to know something deeper about him, needed to know he could be vulnerable, too.

"Tell me about that," she insisted softly.

He hesitated. She thought he might distract with charm. But he didn't. After a long moment, he spoke.

"My dad left my mom and I when I was six." His voice had a roughness around the edge of it that it did not normally have. "My mom was ill. We lived in places smaller than shoeboxes. On one memorable occasion, we lived in a car for three days. Sometimes we went to McDonald's and stole creamers because she didn't have money for milk. She would have considered this wine champagne."

Somehow his revealing this part of himself was

the most extraordinary of gifts. This was authentic, the edge of raw pain in his voice was real. That he had found her worthy of entrusting with this secret part of himself felt like the best thing that had happened to her in a long time.

Maybe even better than that kiss. Well, maybe not.

The moment of feeling he trusted her was extraordinarily brief. "I don't know why I said that," he said with a regretful shake of his head.

"You can trust me with it," she said softly.

"Thanks," he replied, but his tone was clipped.

She had questions, but assumed from the growl in his voice and his use of the past tense when talking about the champagne, that his mother was dead, and that it still caused him pain to think about it.

"Did my dad know how things were for you?" she asked.

He looked like he was very annoyed by the fact she was continuing the conversation, but after a moment he answered.

"Not all the details, but he knew I was shouldering a lot of responsibility. He helped me apply for scholarships at college. He wrote me letters of endorsement. I think he paid me more than I was worth when I worked for him. Your dad was one decent guy, Bree."

"So are you."

He lifted a shoulder.

"I think that's why you're such a decent guy," she said softly. "You know firsthand what it's like to have it tough."

Maybe it was the wrong thing to say, because a veil went down completely in his eyes, as if he regretted sharing the confidence as much as she welcomed it.

"We'll save my tales of woe for a different day," he said smoothly. "Right now I want to hear the rest of yours."

She would have liked to talk about him some more, but she could clearly see he had said all he was going to say for one day. She appreciated his confidence and did not want to appear to pry. So, she took a fortifying gulp of her wine before launching into the rest of the story.

"I thought I could rent another kitchen, but I've been unable to find a suitable space in my price range. I'm behind on orders. You can see I can't work out of here. I'm going to have to cancel the Crystal Silvers contract. And Perks. I'm going to have to let Chelsea go, and she's already a mess, poor kid. I know I will eventually get back on my feet, but for now—" Despite that fortifying gulp of wine her voice cracked.

"For now, I'm done," she choked out. She finished her wine in one long pull. When she went to refill, he took the bottle and put it out of her reach, beside him on the floor.

"Bree, I might be able to help you out."

So, here they were again. He was going to help her out. He still felt as if he owed her dad a debt of gratitude.

But she didn't want to fight it anymore. She was so tired. She just wanted to sink into his strength. To let him take care of her. To let him rescue her from her life. There were worse things than letting a super successful man—who had a good heart and was decent to boot—look after you, take your troubles away.

Okay, so she had taken ten giant steps back from the woman in the beautiful cloak and high heels that she had been just two short days ago. She might never see that woman again, she realized sadly. The cloak was probably going to have to go to a consignment store. She couldn't in good conscience take it back. The dog had slobbered on it.

"You probably have a team of lawyers," she said. "Thank you."

"Wasn't even thinking of the legal aspects of your dilemma, but yes, I'll run your liability issues by my legal eagles."

"What were you thinking about?"

"A place for you to work."

"I appreciate you wanting to help, but believe me," she said, "I've already tried everything. I even hoped maybe I could rent a restaurant kitchen, after hours, work all night if I had to, but I just couldn't turn anything up. Again, it's the budget. And I don't want you to offer to rent me a kitchen over my budget, because the cookie business can't sustain that. It's still a business, not a charity, and if I can't run it in the black—"

"Bree, be quiet."

She sighed. Was he hearing her?

"I have a kitchen," he said softly. "In your price range. I have a commercial kitchen. That's completely empty. And available. That no one ever uses."

"Yeah, as if that would be in my price range."

"It's in your price range."

"You don't even know what my price range is. It's laughably small."

"The kitchen is free."

"Are you kidding me?" She could not keep the skepticism out of her voice. "I would have to hate you forever if you rented a kitchen for me, and then told me it was free out of some kind of misguided—"

"I would never lie to you like that. Never. And I would never risk having you hate me forever."

She could feel herself falling toward the most frightening thing of all: hope. She searched his face. She could see the innate trustworthiness of him. She felt that hope flutter to reluctant life in her chest.

"If you're kidding me, I'll have to kill you. You know that, don't you?"

"I understand completely. I mean, it's just theoretical, because I have a kitchen, but how would you go about killing me?"

"I'd have to think about it," she said regally.

"Because I'm quite big, and you're quite small. It's not like I would just stand there, with my arms open, saying, 'okay, kill me now.' And to be honest, you don't seem very threatening. I think it may be the slippers you took off a while ago that ruin your killer image."

"Maybe those slippers shoot…things. Like in a James Bond movie."

"You'd have to be more specific to convince me. Bullets? Darts? Cookies?"

She loved this bantering back and forth, but she had to know.

"Brand, please do not keep me in suspense another moment! We can discuss your potential demise another time. Tell me about the kitchen! No one *has* a kitchen, just sitting around, at their disposal."

"Well, I do."

Don't get your hopes up, she told herself. She was crying. She couldn't help it. "Where is it? Brand, I need to start right away. I'm so far behind. If I work night and day I might be able to get the Crystal Silvers birthday cookies done. Maybe."

"You'll get them done," he said, with such absolute confidence in her that she cried harder.

"How can I thank you? Where is it?"

"It's at my house."

Her heart dropped, and the tears of relief stopped. She tried not to replace them with the despairing, hopeless kind.

She took a deep breath, and did her best not to sound too skeptical. But she'd already resigned herself to it. It was too good to be true.

"You have a commercial kitchen in your house? No one has a commercial kitchen in their house.

Why would a bachelor have a commercial kitchen in his house?"

"When I bought the house, I renovated it, top to bottom. The designer told me a commercial kitchen was an investment. She said the kind of house I have is where large functions are catered."

Of course he'd have that kind of house. Brand was a billionaire. Still, Bree was a little awestruck all the same.

"I gave my poor designer a pretty hard time about that kitchen. She just kept insisting that someday I'd be really glad I had it. And you know what?"

"What?" Bree breathed.

"She was absolutely right."

His voice was soft and strong at the same time, the voice of a man who could make someone believe, all over again, even when they knew better, that magic was part of the fabric of life, that miracles happened all the time.

That when you had totally given up, when you had no hope left, life could surprise you all over again with how good it could be.

CHAPTER SEVEN

BREE EVANS WAS in his house.

Brand recognized, on the danger scale, the needle was edging toward the top of the red zone.

Because she was so very complex. Adorable. But smart. An astute businesswoman. The daughter of a man who had helped him. A woman whose kiss he could not get out of his head.

He'd confided in her that he'd once lived in a car. No one but his mother knew that about his life. What kind of moment of ridiculous weakness had that been?

Brand watched her race around his kitchen, nearly beside herself with excitement, and it felt as if every ounce of that danger he had invited into his life was worthwhile.

She stopped at the Elvis cookie jar. She took

out a cookie and examined it as if she had found a bug.

"Beau's?" she said.

"He does have a weakness. Despite what Jenn said, I restrict him to one or two a week. He mostly gets dog biscuits, which he only tolerates."

"When I get caught up, I'll try making something for him that's healthier and that he'll love." She put the cookie back in the jar, and examined the jar itself. "Somehow I didn't figure you for an Elvis kind of guy."

The less she figured out about him, the better. Especially now that he had given her hints. Especially now that she was under his roof. Making herself at home.

No, that wasn't quite right. She wasn't making herself at home, she was making it feel like home.

Without even trying. She was making it feel like home even *before* she tried baking cookies for his dog.

"What exactly would you consider an Elvis kind of guy?" he asked, intrigued despite himself.

"Sleazily oversexed?"

"Elvis?" he said, with pretended hurt. "That's slanderous. You have enough legal problems without slandering the King."

"I think e-Us matched me with him once. Complete with the sweaty scarf." She shuddered delicately.

"Okay, here's the deal. I said the kitchen was free, but it's not."

"Don't do this to me," she moaned.

"No more e-Us. That's the price."

"Deal," she said, way too fast.

He eyed her suspiciously.

"I've got my sights set on Kevin."

"I hope you don't."

"I do," she said and whipped her phone out of her back pocket. "Look. There's an app that teaches you to speak Klingon."

He saw she was teasing him. Or he was pretty sure she was teasing him. But she did know about the app.

"I'm going to be way too busy to have a social life," she declared happily.

Why was he happy, too? What did he care about her social life or lack thereof?

She was dashing around the kitchen again, opening drawers, looking in cupboards. She ran reverent hands over one of the ovens. "A steam oven. I could not have dreamed."

She opened it up. "You've never used this," she said with faint accusation.

"How do you know?"

"The racks have cardboard on the corners."

"Oh."

"Three ovens," she whispered, looking around. "Have you used any of them? Oh!" she squealed, before he had a chance to answer. "Look at this!"

He came over to see what was causing such excitement. She had changed out of her pajamas, and put her hair up with a band. He liked the shoestring better, not that he wanted her to know he'd noticed. She was wearing snug jeans and a white top.

She was bent over a lower cabinet looking inside it. He could look at that particular sight for a long time, but it made him feel like an oversexed Elvis so he made himself focus on what she was looking at. Something huge and ugly and red was in his cupboard.

"What is that?" he asked, astounded.

"It's in your kitchen. You don't know?" She tossed an amused look over her shoulder.

"See that thing over there?" he said, and pointed. "It's called a microwave. I know that. And the fridge. I've used the coffeemaker a couple of times."

"That explains why it's so clean in here."

Actually, a cleaning staff kept it clean in here, but it seemed so pretentious to say it, that he didn't.

"Well, this—" she tugged, and the whole shelf slid out and began to rise "—is a stand mixer. Sometimes called a batch mixer."

He was so startled at it moving by itself that he took a step back. He actually took her shoulders and moved her back, too.

The monstrous apparatus rose silently and then stopped at counter level.

"If it moves toward you, run," he whispered.

He loved her giggle. She sounded like Goldie Hawn.

"It's not dangerous," she assured him. She reached out as if she was going to pet it.

He grabbed her hand. "Don't touch. I think it may be HAL."

"HAL?"

She had to ask. He wouldn't break it to her just yet that she didn't have a hope with Kevin. He didn't care about her and Kevin. Shoot. He cared about her and Kevin. And her and some guy who had stiffed her for coffee. And her and the sleazy oversexed guy with the scarf. He was still holding her hand. He dropped it like it was hot.

"2001: A Space Odyssey."

She was all over that ugly red space alien piece of machinery. "I'm not familiar with it."

Kiss Kevin goodbye.

"It's a movie. Old. Sci-fi."

"Hmmm, you don't look like a sci-fi kind of guy."

Or an Elvis kind of guy. He was going to ask her how she knew a sci-fi guy from one who wasn't, but she'd probably dated one.

Instead he said, "I'm not really a sci-fi guy, but when you work with the geek squad, you pick up on what they consider to be the essentials of life. Consider it like being immersed in a continuous episode of *The Big Bang Theory*."

She was very focused on the apparatus in front of her but laughed at his joke. She was obviously very familiar with the ugly red space alien. Was she caressing the damn thing?

Don't ask. "What kind of guy would you say I am?" he asked.

"The best kind," she said with a smile. "The kind with a commercial kitchen *and* a stand mixer."

"I have other sterling qualities."

"Where's your bedroom?"

His jaw dropped. He, who considered himself

virtually unshakable, felt like he was turning the same color as the darned mixer.

"That's not what I meant," he said. His voice sounded like a squeak.

She actually turned her attention away from the attractions of the mixer and stared at him. And then her eyes widened. And then she giggled, that funny little Goldie Hawn giggle. And then the giggle deepened into something even better. She laughed. She laughed until she doubled over from it. She laughed until the tears were squirting out her eyes.

"Oh, my God, Brand."

"What's so damn funny?"

"I wasn't suggesting you had sterling qualities in the bedroom. Not that you don't. I mean maybe you do."

Her laughter dried up, just like that. Now they were both standing there with faces as red as the mixer.

"I'm going to be trying to catch up on my orders." She was speaking very fast, her words tumbling over one another. "I need to call Chelsea.

We'll probably work all night. I wanted to know where your bedroom was so we wouldn't disturb you. So I know how quiet I need to be. We usually work with music. And equipment like this—" she patted that mixer with disturbing affection again "—is quite loud."

"Oh." He said. "That's a relief." Well, kind of a disappointment, but mostly a relief.

She actually looked faintly hurt. "Yes, isn't it?"

"My bedroom's a long way away. Play anything you want. As loud as you want."

"Do you have a favorite Elvis song?"

The soundtrack of his childhood. He could tell from which one was playing when he walked through the door after school how his Mom was going to be that evening. Or maybe more accurately, who she was going to be.

He could have never told Wendy about that. Had never wanted to.

And yet, at this precise moment, there was an ache to tell Bree. It felt as if he would die of loneliness if he didn't tell her.

But he didn't.

Instead, he forced his tone to be smooth and light, and answered, "Must I pick only one? Impossible. Yours?"

She didn't hesitate. "'I Can't Help—'"

She stopped. She stared at him. She stammered, "Uh, I can't think of one. 'Jailhouse Rock' maybe."

He should tell her never to take up poker. She was a terrible liar.

They were definitely in the danger zone right now, right this instant. He could feel the chemistry between them. The needle was edging up into red. He'd made a mistake inviting her into his space. He could clearly see that.

"Don't worry about disturbing me at all," he said. "I was just going to pack a bag, anyway."

"You were?"

"Yes, I have a business trip. We're opening a new physical location. Bali." He hadn't been planning on going to the opening until thirty seconds ago. Suddenly it felt imperative to put a world of oceans between them.

"Bali," she said.

He thought of her in Bali. Carefree. He wondered if she'd ever snorkeled. Or surfed. That was where he had learned to do both. He felt an unfortunate curiosity about what she would look like in a bikini.

"Okay," he said, hastily "if you've got everything you need, I'll go pack."

"Yes," she said formally. "I've taken enough of your time."

He moved away from her, edging toward the door. Edging back toward the world where he controlled everything. Where there were surprises, of course there were, but in a way, even though they were surprises, they were predictable kind of surprises. Like deciding to go to Bali on a moment's notice.

Nothing that made his heart do what it was doing right now.

Thank goodness!

"Yes, you do that," she said, as insultingly eager to get rid of him as he was to go. "Go to pack. Do I need a key? To get in and out? I'll need to go for supplies."

He started to say he didn't lock it. But suddenly he didn't want his house unlocked with him away and her coming in and out. What if she was coming in with her arms full of groceries and there was an intruder, already inside? Or what if she was inside making a bunch of noise, so much noise she might not hear an intruder? Beau would be left at the office while he was away. Should he leave him here with her instead? To protect her?

No. The dog would probably compromise the health standards of the kitchen. There was a keypad on the front door that Brand had never used. He was going to have to figure it out. He'd call one of his technical geniuses.

It occurred to him he'd never thought he had anything of value in here. It was valuable stuff, but he recognized, right this minute, he had no attachment to any of it.

It felt as if Bree Evans was the only valuable thing in his world.

Her and Beau.

Beau could look after himself.

"I have to get going," he said again. He could hear the desperation in his own voice. He was pretty sure there was a line of sweat breaking out over his top lip.

She waltzed over to him. She looked as if she was going to kiss him again. He backed away from her rapidly.

"Make yourself at home while I'm away," Brand said. "If you need a break there's a media room through that door. The freezer has microwavable stuff in it, if you get sick of eating cookies. There are guest bedrooms upstairs if you need a snooze. There's four, no, five powder rooms, so take your pick."

There was that look again, as if she might kiss him. He backed away from her even more rapidly. As unmanly as it was, he was practically running from her.

"Thank you," she called after him, as he went through the door to the hallway.

Her voice sounded as if it had laughter in it. Minx. She *liked* making him uncomfortable.

And he liked making her laugh. In fact, Brand

was very aware that a man could live to make her laugh, to wipe the worry lines from her forehead, to erase the sorrow from her eyes…

A better man than him, he reminded himself. One without baggage, a ragtag excuse for a family, a number of failed forays into the relationship department, his only serious one, Wendy, having failed quite colossally.

Bali, he told himself. That should take his mind off her. Sand and surf and work. Lots and lots of work.

Work. It had always been the place he escaped. It was a world where a person could apply their mind to problems and make them dissolve. It was a world where the challenges were not personal, where they had no emotion attached to them. It was a world he could lose himself in, shut out any little thing that bothered him or caused him distress or discomfort.

The only thing was, he'd never been aware before that he used it to escape the nebulous unsolvable kind of problems that popped up when you became attached to another person.

He waited until he was out of the house to slide his phone from his pocket. He punched in the familiar number. He got her answering message.

"Hi, Mom, I'm going to be away for a couple of days. I'll video-call you tonight on your phone."

His mother loved that feature on her phone. "It's just like being on *The Jetsons*," she'd say with wonder every single time he called.

CHAPTER EIGHT

BREE CAME AWAKE with a start and a little shriek.

"Sorry, I didn't mean to startle you."

His voice wrapped around her in the darkness and made her feel safe.

"Brand?" she asked sleepily. In what context would she be waking up to Brand? It was a dream, obviously, a delightful dream that she never wanted to end.

"I had no idea you were in here," he said, softly, his voice like the touch of a silk scarf across the back of her neck.

She remembered, slowly, she was in one of the deep recliner chairs in his media room. She had helped herself to one of the Icelandic wool blankets artfully placed in a huge basket in one of the corners.

"What time is it?" You could never tell in the

media room, because, unlike the kitchen, which was saturated in light from the banks of windows, light had been deliberately blocked out of this room.

"Eight."

"In the morning?" she asked, shocked.

"Yeah."

"Are you just getting home?"

"Yeah. I was going to unwind from the trip in here for a bit, but I'll—"

"No—no, of course you can unwind in your own home. Chelsea and I finished late. It was about two in the morning. I should have gone home," she said, suddenly embarrassed. "I was just going to sit here for a moment, but I made the mistake of reclining the chair. So comfy! I hope I didn't leave the ovens on." She sniffed the air. "I wouldn't want to burn down two kitchens."

"There's nothing burning. The house smells incredible, though. You could bottle that smell. Make a fortune."

Her eyes were adjusting to the dark. He was still dressed for the tropics in light pants and a sports shirt. He looked so yummy, ever so slightly travel-rumpled, his hair not quite as crisply groomed as normal, his cheeks and chin dark with whisker stubble.

She remembered she had on the white-net baking cap, and she tried to remove it as surreptitiously as possible and stuff it in the pocket of her chef's jacket. Why did he always have to catch her at her worst?

"How was Bali?"

He didn't answer.

"Not what you hoped?" she asked. "Did something go wrong?"

"No, not really. I'm just a bit off. Time difference." He moved by her, took the deep chair next to hers and pushed it back into full recline. "Anything new in the fire investigation?"

Bree cast Brand a glance out of the corner of her eye. His hands were folded over his stomach and he was looking at the ceiling. It had been a week since she'd seen him. Was he deliberately avoiding talking about himself?

"Chelsea's a mess. She's been interviewed twice, and they've intimidated her horribly."

"Does she have a lawyer?"

"On what I pay her?"

"Would you let me look after it?"

A terrible tenderness unfolded in her at the weariness etched into the lines of his handsome face. Of course she felt tender toward him! He had saved her business. He had given her a place to work that was beyond her wildest dreams. Now he was offering to help Chelsea.

"Thank you," she said, feeling any defenses she had left against him crumbling as she accepted his gift with the graciousness it deserved. "You should go to bed."

"You should, too."

Together. She knew the renegade thought proved she was not just feeling tender toward him because of her business or his offer to help Chelsea.

"I think I'm awake for the day," she said hastily, to move the talk and her still dream-weakened thoughts away from the topic of beds.

"Yes, me, too. The worst thing I could do this morning is indulge my desire to sleep. I need to force myself back on to this time."

It reminded her, no matter how tender she felt toward him, that her feelings had to remain her closely guarded secret. They were from different worlds. He was a man accustomed to dealing with jet lag, business trips to Bali and beyond. She made cookies for a living.

"How did the cookies go?" he asked, as if he could read her mind. He asked it as though he really cared, damn him, and as if there was not a huge gap in their socioeconomic circumstances.

"We're completely caught up. All my regular orders are done. Perks got their first order. Chelsea took the Crystal Silvers order to the airport last night when we finished."

"You've been busy," he said.

"Yes, my poor cat has been feeling neglected." Now why had she said that? Add crazy cat lady to cookie maker! Besides, it wasn't true. Her neighbor, an elderly lady, loved Oliver and had liked nothing more than taking the cat while Bree put in these long hours.

"I guess you probably feel the same about Beau? Will you pick him up and bring him home today?"

"I'll probably banish him while the baking is going on. I think your health standard would be compromised by his presence."

"Aw, poor guy."

"Not really. He's used to me being away. He's got a pretty nice setup at the office, too. There's people working there all the time."

"Your office runs all the time?"

"It's that creative-brain thing. Lots of my people say they work best at night. I just go with it. The office is open twenty-four hours. I let them keep track of their own time."

"You need more cookies if you're running twenty-four hours," she said. "Your office is next on the list. I've been filling orders in between the Crystal Silvers special order, and I'm caught up. Your office will be going into the rotation starting on Monday."

"You haven't sent me a contract yet," he said. His voice was husky with sleepiness.

She wouldn't tell him this just yet, because he was sure to reject it, but she wasn't sending him a contract. She was baking his office cookies for free, for the rest of her life. And cookies for Beau, too, as soon as she figured out a dog-friendly recipe.

His chest was starting to rise and fall.

"You can bring Beau home," she said. "I'll be taking the next two days off."

She realized she wanted to stay here forever, feeling warm and safe and oddly happy. She forced herself to throw back the blanket and get up. "Can I bring you anything before I leave?"

"Sure. A Love Bite and a Decadent."

He remembered things. That was the nature of being a businessman, remembering details about people and their businesses. Still, she felt inordinately pleased that he remembered the names of her cookies.

Then he added, "And with anyone else, a decadent love bite would mean something quite different than it does with you. Just saying."

She laughed, a bit uneasily. There it was again, between them, teasing, which was wonderful, but it was teasing with some finely held tension, like a shiver when you went outside on a cold day. "I'll be right back."

But he got up and followed her into the kitchen.

"I don't want to go to sleep," Brand insisted. "I know from past experience what giving in to that temptation does. It can take weeks to get back to normal if you don't force yourself back into a regular daily schedule right away."

Morning light was streaming in the kitchen windows. In the brightness, he still looked tired, and also sexily roguish with that hint of whisker shadow on his face. She could see his skin had picked up a faint golden glow from the sun.

She felt something tingle along her spine. There was something about the way he was looking at her that could give that expression, about giving in to temptation, many meanings. They had been apart for a week. It had not cooled the way she felt about him. It had intensified it.

Did he feel the same way? Or was it all just banter to him? He would be good at flirting, probably with no awareness of how good he was at it. In one sentence of that *City* article they had called him Vancouver's most eligible bachelor.

"Wow," he said, looking around. "If there's a heaven this is what it looks and smells like."

She looked around and saw what he saw. His kitchen was, indeed, a beautiful sight. It was bright and clean, with clearly defined workstations. But the best sight of all—well, besides him—was those big clearly labeled rectangular bakery boxes, stacked up on racks in the center island. Cookies all boxed up and ready to go to their various destinations and drop-off points.

"I'm interested in what brought you to filling up your life with cookies," he said as she handed him the two flavors he had requested. Their fingertips brushed. Something electrical, like static, leaped between them.

It was probably from the Icelandic wool!

"I don't usually recommend these for breakfast," she said, as if she could chase away the electricity, and the helpless feeling it gave her, with stern words.

"Ah, well, its suppertime in Bali." He popped a whole cookie in his mouth—no easy task—then closed his eyes and chewed contentedly.

"They aren't healthy for supper, either!"

Though watching him, a memory tickled the back of her mind.

"My dad used to eat them for supper sometimes," she said softly, then added thoughtfully, "I guess that's the *why* of cookies. I got an Easy-Bake Oven for Christmas when I was six, and was soon tired of the limitations of it. I graduated to the big-girl oven and started baking cookies for my dad. If there were cookies, warm out of the oven, when he got home, he'd get so excited. He'd gobble them down for supper. He'd do impressions of the Cookie Monster until my mother and I were in hysterics, rolling on the floor, begging him to stop. Of course, it just egged him on.

"The base dough for those cookies you are eating right now is the recipe I kept working on as a kid. It still changes slightly from time to time. For instance, last year, I started adding a bit of coffee to it."

"Good business," Brand said, opening his eyes and regarding her. "Coffee and chocolate, highly addictive."

"I never gave that a thought."

"You wouldn't," he said.

If he was going to insist on seeing her as an innocent, she was going to have to kiss him again.

No! She could never kiss him again. Because it made her long for things she could not have.

He was so far out of her league it wasn't even funny.

"I haven't just been making cookies. I've been looking for another kitchen. I can't impose on you forever. I think I've got a line on one. It sounds as if it might be available for the beginning of the month. Beau can come home."

"Sheesh, stop feeling guilty about Beau."

"I've displaced him. And you, too."

"This is pretty normal for me. To travel. To be away for long periods."

"Do you ever stay still?" she asked quietly. "Do you ever just kick back and enjoy your beautiful home?"

"Oh, sure," he said. "I wind down here. You've seen the media room. It's perfect for football and a beer."

"That's not actually what I meant," she said.

"Oh? What did you mean?"

"I meant…" She tried to think of how to put it. "I meant a fire in the fireplace. And a turkey in the oven. A Christmas tree."

"It's May!" he said.

"I'm not explaining it very well." She was *not* explaining it very well, but she also suspected he was being deliberately obtuse.

"No, you're not."

"It's not about Christmas. It's about a feeling. Of being *home*."

"Cue the *Little House on the Prairie* music," he said sarcastically.

But, in actual fact, she already knew this about

him: his space lacked a sense of being a home. It was as if the house had spoken to her while he'd been away, divulged some of his secrets.

It was a beautiful house, like the houses you saw in magazines. She had taken advantage of his invitation and in his absence she had napped in one of the gorgeous upstairs bedrooms. She had found excuses to inspect all the powder rooms.

Everything was perfect, as perfect and as high-end as the kitchen would have you predict it would be. There were beautiful original art pieces, priceless hand-knotted rugs, painted silk wallpapers, incredible one-of-a-kind light fixtures and the aforementioned hand-knitted Icelandic throws. There were collectibles from many different countries, artfully worked into the décor. The furniture was all stunning. There were gorgeous scenes all over the house, as if they were waiting for a photographer. A desk with a leather-bound journal open and a pen beside it in an alcove under an upstairs window. A fireplace in the formal living room with the fire laid, as if all you had to do was strike a match. There were two vases of spring fresh tulips on a long dining room table that looked as if it had never been eaten at. There were fresh rosebuds in all the guest bedrooms, and a bucket full of delicately blushing pink peonies in the landing of the grand staircase.

And yet, as almost overwhelmingly beautiful as everything was, and despite how busy and how exhausted Bree was, she thought that his house felt empty. Staff came in, to clean and change flowers, but that just made it feel even more like a house that was being beautifully staged to sell, rather than a house anyone lived in.

There was no sign of his entertaining female guests, either. There was no second toothbrush, no tubes of mascara left out, no feminine shoes in the front coat closet, no chick flicks in his enormous collection of movies, no yogurt or diet soda in his fridge.

She felt as if the house cried for the feminine touches that would have made it a home and for children screaming and running up and down the halls and leaving messes everywhere. It felt as if the house longed for laughter, love, energy.

It felt as if the house wanted to be filled up with the smells of people living in it: roast beef in the oven, crisp Yorkshire puddings erupting out of baking tins.

It was the saddest thing she could think of: a house that had never had cookies baked in it, or at least not while he had lived here. She could tell none of the three ovens had ever been used. The state-of-the-art appliances all sparkled prettily, but, like the stoves, she would put money on whether or not they had ever been turned on until she came along.

And even now, it was the scent of cookie *production*, not cookies, that had welcomed him back from his trip.

That is what she was very aware of. It was a house. Not a home. A place to crash and watch a football game and drink a beer.

Instead of making her feel awed by his success, the house had made her feel the acute loneliness of it. She understood perfectly why he would not spend a great deal of time here, or be eager to come "home" to it.

The only room she truly liked was the media room, with its deep, ugly chairs, and its stinky dog bed, and its gaudy Elvis posters and its faint smell of old popcorn.

Underneath Brand's sarcastic tone—"cue the *Little House on the Prairie* music"—Bree heard the faintest thing: a longing, a wistfulness.

All of a sudden she knew she wasn't leaving right away, even though that would be the smartest thing to do, even though her cat had suffered enough neglect this week.

If she wanted to protect her poor heart, and she did, she should already be halfway out that door.

But suddenly, it was not all about her. Suddenly, she was aware that was not how she had been raised. She was almost ashamed of the self-centeredness that wanted her to protect herself when she had the most precious gift to give this man who had done so much for her.

She had discovered what she could give him. This man who had saved her business, casually, as if it meant nothing, as if life was a game of

Monopoly and he had a pocket full of save-a-business-for-free cards.

She wanted to repay him. But how did you repay a man who had everything? You gave him the one thing he had never had.

She could give him something he had missed. She knew from the small snippets of his childhood that he had confided in her about—living in a car for three days, for goodness sake—that it was unlikely his home had held normal activities, like baking cookies.

Giving him cookies for life was not enough. Besides, they were material. He could buy warehouses full of cookies. Her cookies, or someone else's. She'd been in this business long enough to know competition was stiff and rapidly growing. Hers was not the only company that produced a delicious, meticulously made product.

So, she could give Brand the experience of *making* cookies. A piece of a missing childhood. A magic piece. A sense of what that place called *home* could feel like.

"Have you ever made cookies?" she asked him.

"No, never." He confirmed what she had already guessed, but he looked wary.

"Let's change that. Right now."

"No, you're tired. Go home."

But she wasn't going to go home. Now that she had figured out the gift she could give him, it felt imperative to do it now. Maybe because he was tired, his defenses were down a little bit.

Because really? Under normal circumstances what billionaire was going to spend a morning baking cookies?

But he cocked his head at her, reluctantly interested. He lifted a shoulder in assent.

"Do I need one of those?" he asked, gesturing at her chef's jacket.

"Only if you're worried about your shirt." She shrugged out of her own. "We're not baking commercially right now. We're making a single batch of my original-recipe chocolate-chip cookies. For you."

"Do they have magic in them?" he asked softly.

"Oh, I hope so," she responded, just as softly. And then, she moved away from the intensity building between them. She moved, instead, over to her iPod station.

"Want some music?" she asked.

"Sure."

She found an Elvis Presley hits playlist and started it, then glanced back at him. "What?"

"Maybe not Elvis this morning."

There was something in his face, guarded and yet vulnerable. There was some secret about him and Elvis he was not yet willing to divulge.

Yet. The word suggested her subconscious was already looking to a future her rational mind knew was not possible.

She changed the setting to random. She supposed, if he listened, her music selection was going to say as much about her as his house did about him.

Romantic. Hope-filled. Longing for love.

"Okay," she said brightly, hoping to distract him from the telling messages of her music choices. "Let's start. Cookies 101."

"Do I have to touch HAL? I don't think I can touch HAL."

She giggled at his pretended fear of the mixer. "I was thinking something a little more old-fashioned. A big bowl. A wooden spoon, some basic ingredients. And my secrets."

"I want to know your secrets," he said huskily, "especially if they involve a wooden spoon."

He was tired. She was tired. They had to tread very carefully here, so she ignored his playful, suggestive innuendo, even as she filed it away. *He's seeing me as a grown-up. You don't say things like that to someone you think of as a kid.*

"Secret number one, coming right up." She went to the fridge, reached in and held the tinfoil packet out to him with showmanship.

"Butter," he said. He lifted his eyebrows at her. How could a man say so much without saying a single word?

"Stop it!"

"I never said anything."

"I know. That's a special talent, being so bad without saying a word."

One eyebrow stayed up as the other went down. It was a very sexy look.

"You're being very wicked," she said sternly.

"Yes, I am," he said, not a bit contrite. "I think people usually use oil, but butter might—"

"You need to stop it." The protest was token. Again, she felt a little tingle. He was definitely seeing her as a woman! That decision to show him some magic was having consequences much more dangerous than she could have imagined. She didn't feel anything like a Girl Guide doing a good deed!

She wondered exactly what she had let herself in for.

And the truth was she couldn't wait to find out!

"There is no wickedness in cookie making," she told him sternly.

"Yes, ma'am, no wickedness in cookie making." He repeated it dutifully. The way he said *wickedness*, with so much heat, could melt an iceberg!

"Butter, real butter, no imitations, is the number-one secret to making good cookies," she said primly, as if his teasing was not making her feel alive and happy. She could feel the laughter bubbling up inside of her. Of course, if she laughed, there would be no stopping him. She had not anticipated this particular problem when she had thought of giving the gift of some childhood magic to a fully grown man.

She had to ignore his sexiness. If she didn't, she would teach him nothing about home, and underscore his ability to distract. She had wanted it to be fun, yes, but she could not succumb to his charm, or fun was going to take an unexpected turn that had nothing to do with her original motivation in extending this invitation.

"You need to pay attention." She said it out loud to herself, a reminder to stay focused on cookies and not the dark tangle of his lashes, the sensual curve of his bottom lip, the way his light pants clung to the large muscles of his thighs.

"Will there be a test?" he asked solemnly.

Focusing hard, she unwrapped the butter from its tinfoil and put it in a small bowl. Her fingers felt clumsy under his gaze, as if she had dipped them in glue that had hardened. She turned from him and softened the butter in the microwave. "Thirty seconds," she told him, "just enough for it to slide out."

"Slide out," he repeated as if he was being an obedient student, which he was not! He made the words sound like something out of the *Kama Sutra*!

She shoved the two-cup measure at him. "One of white sugar, two of brown."

She cast a glance at him a minute later after the room had descended into total silence. His tongue was caught between his teeth. His focus was intense.

"You're not measuring gunpowder."

"You're the one who stripped all the fun out of it already."

"I did not."

"I'm surprised you didn't tell me I can't use the word *stripped.* As well as not speaking of anything wicked."

"For heaven's sake, I am not a complete stick-in-the-mud!"

"Okay. When's the last time you had fun, since you brought it up?"

"This *is* fun for me."

"But you are not a complete stick-in-the-mud,"

he said sadly. “An example of fun that has nothing to do with cookies. Tell me the last thing that made you laugh.”

The last things that had made her laugh all involved him. Nearly. “I bought a laser pointer. My cat chases the red dot.”

He was silent.

“Obsessively.”

He remained silent.

“It’s much funnier than you think.”

“You need to get out more.”

Her sense of deep gratitude to him, and of wanting to give him a gift, was dissipating quite rapidly.

“We can’t all spend our lives frolicking on beaches, turning that lovely shade of gold that you are right now.”

“You do look a little pale,” he said, regarding her solemnly. “Jailhouse pallor. Chained to the kitchen too long. You need to get outside.”

“Thank you. If you could measure the brown—”

“If you did frolic on a beach, would it be in a bikini or a one-piece?”

CHAPTER NINE

SHOOT, BRAND THOUGHT. There it was, out of his mouth. The whole time he'd been in Bali he'd wondered that. Bikini or one-piece? Bali had not been quite the escape that he had hoped for. Now, here he was in the kitchen with Bree, being as wicked as baking cookies allowed, and somehow the question had just popped out of his mouth.

Bree's mouth fell open. She looked flustered.

Well, who could blame her? He was tired. He should have never agreed to the cookie-making session.

He knew what it was really about. She had seen something in him, sensed something in this house. A longing. A vulnerability. He was going to distract her from her quest.

Which was what? To know the real him?

That, yes, but more. She was determined to show him something he had missed.

Her motivations, he was one-hundred-percent positive, were nothing but altruistic. He should have never let it slip about living in the car, about his childhood being less than ideal, because she was busy filling in the gaps now. The problem was, once you had been shown something like that, didn't you then ache for it forever?

He did not want to be thinking of the word *forever* anywhere in the vicinity of her.

"Why don't you guess?" she suggested, her cheeks pink.

His distractions, he was pleased to see, were working. He had entirely removed the focus from himself.

"I'm going to guess a one-piece—"

"That's correct."

"When it should be a bikini."

"Four eggs," she said, a little too loudly. She held up a device in her hand. "This is a handheld electric mixer. Think of it as HAL's little sister. We're going to whip the butter."

"Look, if you don't want any wickedness you can't talk about whips."

She put her hands on her hips. "I hope you aren't that kind of guy, Brand Wallace." Sternly, she handed him the electric beaters. "Put them in the butter and sugar and turn them on. That should drown out the sound of your voice."

"I'm offended," he said, though he was not. In the least.

"Aside from butter, this is the secret to making really, really good cookies."

"Good whipping?" he said innocently.

She pinched her lips together. It didn't help one little bit. The laughter gurgled out past her closed lips.

He'd totally succeeded in distracting her from the topic of himself.

And he had totally failed to protect himself.

Because her laughter was a balm to a life that suddenly came face-to-face with the emptiness of all his accomplishments and all his stuff. He had somehow missed the most important thing of all.

Connection.

She laughed until she doubled over, until tears ran down her face.

It made him realize he knew secrets about her, too, that she probably did not want him to know.

Despite her laughter right now, there was some sadness in her that would not let her go, that had not been in her when he had escorted her to her prom. She had been shy, yes, and awkward, yes, but almost filled to the brim with an innocent confidence life would be good to her. He wondered, not for the first time, what might have happened to her.

Don't go there, he ordered himself. *Keep it light. You don't want to go deep with her. You'll be drowning in the pools of light that are her incredible eyes before you even know you're in trouble.*

That was the whole problem, wasn't it? He wasn't that kind of guy, there was nothing twisted or kinky about him. Not even close. But he was not the kind of guy that a girl like her needed, either. As long as both of them were playing by the same rules, as long as both of them remembered that.

"All I am is the kind of guy who likes to make a pretty girl blush."

"I'm not blushing." She was trying to stop laughing. She was blushing with the intensity of a house on fire. She had unbent herself and was cracking eggs into the cookie mixture as if her life depended on it. "Keep, er, mixing it."

As he mixed, she slowly added flour and other ingredients. She was standing close to him, and he could look down on her hair, her gorgeous sunshine-on-sand hair. Would it get lighter if she frolicked on a beach?

The dough began to take on the texture of thick peanut butter.

It was such a blatant lie, about her blushing, that he laughed. Her face, from laughter and racy undertones to the conversation, was nearly as red as the stand mixer.

"And I'm not that pretty, either," she said quietly.

"What? What the hell?" His own laughter died.

So did his resolution not to go there, to her secrets, to her sadness, to some place that had stolen the confidence that had just begun to bloom in her when he had taken her to her prom, a lifetime ago.

"I'm not," she said firmly.

"What would make you say something like that?"

"Maybe I'm adorable, like a Yorkie," she said. "But I know I'm not the greatest. All those guys—the ones I meet on e-Us? They never call me back. Not even the Elvis look-alike."

"That's impossible," he said grimly.

"I have an affliction."

Good grief! "An affliction? Like you're dying or something?" He could not believe how his heart stopped in his chest.

"Oh, for Pete's sake," she said. She actually flicked a piece of cookie batter at him. "Of course I'm not dying."

He tried not to let his relief show. He scraped the dough off his shirt and licked his finger. He was aware of her eyes on him. He took his time licking his finger. The dough was delicious.

"The affliction?" he reminded her, not allowing himself to be distracted by the deliciousness of the dough, as difficult as that was.

"Even growing up," she said slowly, "I knew exactly what I wanted. It was so ordinary and old-fashioned. My girlfriends wanted to be doctors and lawyers, writers and scientists. Oh, sure, they wanted to get married, and have families, but it was like an afterthought. I'll win the Pulitzer Prize, *then* I'll have a baby.

"But my happiest moments were when my family was together, raking leaves, or sitting beside the fire on a cold night, all reading our books. I loved plain moments—arguing over whether it was really a word in Scrabble, or my dad trying to explain football to me, yet again."

It was that *thing* that he had worried about. That she was painting pictures of all the things he had never had, and it could create an ache in him that would never ease.

"I felt safe and cherished—"

Things he had never felt, except maybe with Beau. He was pretty sure that made him, the guy who had been named businessman of the decade, and who had just returned to his beautiful home from a business trip in Bali, pathetic. But this was not about him.

"And that's all I ever wanted for my future. To feel that way, forever."

"And?" He had to force himself to ask the question, because she was taking him on a journey that he did not have a map for. He did not like journeys without maps.

"When my dad died I wanted it even *more*."

"That seems pretty natural."

"I can't *make* it happen." Now that she had started, it felt like the floodgates were wide open. "I'm plagued by first-date anxiety so strong I never get a second one."

"You're getting a terrifying look on your face," he told her, and it was true.

"A terrifying look?" she asked, all innocence.

"As in you want a first date that leads to a second date, and then a third one."

"And?"

"And then wedding bells and babies."

He hadn't thought she could blush any deeper than when he'd been teasing her while whipping the cookies, but she could.

"I had no idea I was so transparent!"

"Believe me, on the transparency scale? You are a perfect ten."

"My only perfect ten," she said glumly.

"That's not true."

"Anyway, I can't help it if my dreams are written all over me. It seems deceitful to not let it be known upfront what your end goal is. I mean why lead someone to believe I'm into casual—"

The fiery burn moving up her cheeks increased, if that was possible. No wonder her kitchens caught fire. She managed to avoid using the word *sex*.

"Casual relationships when nothing could be further from the truth."

"It seems to me if that dream is what you really wanted, you'd already have it because not all guys are as terrified by such dreams as me."

"Well, as I told you, I have an affliction."

"That wasn't it?" he asked. "Wanting babies and weddings and forever?"

She scowled at him. "No."

"Okay, give. About the affliction."

"I get nervous," she confessed.

"Who doesn't get nervous on a first date? That's hardly an affliction."

She sighed.

"I guess you better give me an example."

"I blurt out dumb things. I sweat in my dress. I've steamed up my glasses, and gotten dust under my contact lenses. I've spilled my wine. And dribbled food down my front. Once, I broke a tooth and I had to find an emergency dental clinic. And he didn't even help me.

"It's like I have that terrible affliction like the one golfers get. Where they start whiffing or flubbing or whatever it's called, and once they start thinking about it, they can't get over it. It just gets worse and worse and worse."

She had been focusing hard on the cookie

dough. She looked up at him. Her eyes were wide and earnest.

He could feel his lips twitching. Anyone who did business with him, or worked with him on a regular basis, knew it was not a good thing.

But she, innocent that she was, looked puzzled. "Are you laughing at me?"

"Laughing? No! I'm feeling really annoyed with you." The truth was, he wanted to kiss the living daylights out of her, because she had so badly lost who she really was and had painted herself into such a corner of self-deceit.

"What? Why?"

"Because you are believing this line of crap that you are telling yourself. And you know what I'd like to know? What's really going on? What's really made you so afraid of your own happiness?"

He inserted a word between *your* and *happiness* that was the universal song of displeasure and that meant "I am dead serious. Do not try and snow me."

CHAPTER TEN

BREE STARED AT BRAND. How had things gone so terribly off the rails? She was supposed to be helping *him*. She had entered his kitchen with the naivety of a Girl Guide thinking she was doing her good deed for the day.

How had he turned things around like this?

And how could it possibly feel as if she *had* to tell him, as if to carry this burden alone for one more second would be to be crushed under the weight of it?

How could it possibly feel as if he had unlocked some secret that she had hidden, even from herself? That somehow she was so afraid she was sabotaging her own dreams?

Could that be true? She grabbed a bag of chocolate chips and began to dump them in the bowl. She should have passed him the wooden spoon, but she felt the need to blow off the energy building in her. She started to mash those chips into the cookie dough, when really it should have been a nice, gentle blending motion.

"It was a man," Brand said softly.

She risked a glance at him. He was regarding her with narrowed eyes, flashing dangerously now, with something that was not mischief. He took the spoon from her and began to pummel the cookie dough with barely leashed aggravation.

"How could you know that?" she whispered.

"I can tell by looking at you," he said. "Some evil bastard broke your heart."

You could never, ever forget this about Brand, not even when you were baking cookies, that he was a keen observer, that he saw things that would remain hidden to those not quite as astute.

Don't tell him, she begged herself. And yet, it felt that if she told him, if she finally said these dreadful things out loud, she would be free in some way. She would solve a puzzle that had mystified her. He already knew anyway. He had guessed it.

"As you know, my dad died shortly after my prom," she said tiredly. "I had already been accepted at college, and I knew he would want me to go.

"But I was extremely vulnerable. I was grieving. My mom had already moved on, already made a decision to sell our house, all of which shocked me and left me with a sense of my whole world disintegrating. I had never spent time away from home before, or lived on my own. One of my professors took an interest in me. It doesn't take a psychiatrist to know I was trying desperately to replace my father's love with the affection of this older man.

"I actually was so naive that I thought my father was in heaven looking after me, that he had sent me this man to ease my broken heart."

Bree had been focusing intently on the cookie dough, but some small sound coming from Brand made her glance up.

The fury in his face might have been a frightening thing if it was directed at her. But it was not.

"Go on," Brand said tersely.

"I found out how much I really meant to him when I discovered I was pregnant."

Brand groaned, a growl of fury and frustration so pure it was almost animal-like. But his voice was soft when he said, "Aw, Bree."

"Even though the pregnancy was the end of my love affair, and I felt I had to leave school so as never to see Paul again, I was happy about the baby. It made me feel not quite so alone in the world. It made me feel as if I had purpose and meaning.

"And then," she whispered, "the baby was gone, too. I miscarried."

She felt his arms go around her. Ever so gently, Brand turned her into his chest. He held her hard and tight. He held her as if there was one solid thing in the world for her to hold onto. He held her in a way that made her finally let go.

At first it was a small hiccup. And then a sob. And then the floodgates opened, and she leaned hard into his strength and his warmth and his acceptance.

"When you told me you knew a thing or two

about unforgivable, that day Beau knocked you over, you were right. Really right. And I'm so sorry you had to experience something like that."

That he remembered something she had said, almost casually, days and days ago, released something more in her.

Brand stroked her hair and her back, and whispered to her over and over again, gentle words of pure compassion.

"Let it go, sweetheart. That's my girl. Get it all out."

And she did. She cried until she was exhausted from it, until there was not a tear left, until surely a different man would have given up holding her a long time ago.

But, no, Brand Wallace stood there like a rock—her rock, immovable in his utter strength.

And when the tears finally did stop, Bree felt something she had not felt for a long, long time.

She felt utterly at peace with herself.

"Thank you for listening," she said. "You've given me some things to think about, self-sabotage for one."

She pulled away from him. His summer shirt had a big splotch on the front of it. She turned to the big bowl of cookie dough. "I think we should just throw this out. I don't think tears make a good secret ingredient."

"I disagree completely," he said. "I think healing is the secret ingredient. Let's bake them and see what happens."

And so, side by side, they scooped dough onto the sheets. She had done it millions of times, and so her cookies were uniform and all the same size.

His were haphazard heaps that made her smile. He made big cookies and small ones and lopsided ones, and she found herself loving all those imperfections. And loving being with him. Was it because she had shared her most secret of secrets that she felt so connected to him? So safe? So comfortable?

But not just comfortable. Aware. Maybe even aware in a way she had not allowed herself to be aware since Paul.

Of Brand's masculinity, in contrast to her femininity. Of his physical size and strength in comparison to herself, of how she had fit against him, of how he smelled, and of his energy.

They put in the cookies to bake, and there was quiet between them as they cleaned up the kitchen, but it was in no way uncomfortable. In fact it was quite lovely, something Bree was aware she had not felt for a long, long time.

It was exactly the gift she had intended to give him, but as was the way with most gifts, she received it herself. Bree had a sense of being home after a long journey away.

The timer rang on the cookies, and she pulled them out of the oven and then she and Brand filled a plate with cookies so warm that chocolate was oozing out of them. Without speaking about it, they both knew where to go, and they retreated to side-by-side chairs in his media room.

She nibbled on one cookie, aware it was his enjoyment that made it the best batch of cookies she had ever made. He ate every one of those cookies they had put on the plate.

And she hoped he was right, that the strange

ingredient—tears—had put healing in them. Because just as he had seen so clearly that there was something broken in her, she also saw that in him.

Maybe what had just happened had strengthened some bond between them. Maybe he would share confidences with her, too.

But he fell asleep with crumbs from the last cookie still in his hand. She brushed them away from him and placed the soft wool blanket, the one that she had used earlier, on him.

She tucked it around him, and took advantage of the fact he was sleeping to study him: the sweep of thick lashes on his cheek, the strong nose, the full lips gently parted, his hair, dark as those melted chocolate chips, just touching his forehead. There was something soft in his face that made her realize how guarded he was most of the time.

All that boyish charm hid something deeper. Something he didn't want anyone to see.

But she had seen it. And as he had said in her apartment that day, it was impossible to "unsee" it now.

He was a man who had absolutely everything. Every material gift that it was possible to own, he owned.

He owned cars, and art pieces and a beautiful house in one of the most exclusive neighborhoods in the world.

And yet, the most precious things of all had evaded him. Children screaming up the staircases, and the Scrabble board open on a table, with a misspelled word on it. Heaps of leaves to leap in, and tying the Christmas tree to the roof with string so it wouldn't fall off. The smell of dinner in the oven, or cookies, the little arguments over whether the toilet-paper roll should unroll over or under. All the simple, complex, wonderful things that went into a home and a family he had missed.

Knowing this with her soul, Bree felt something for him so deep and so stirring that it made her want to weep all over again.

She bent over him, touched his warm, rough cheek, and then followed where her fingertips had been with her lips.

She knew exactly what was happening to her.

It was like the words of that tender Elvis song had crept around her from the first moment she had walked in this house and seen the kitchen where he used the microwave and didn't even know he had a stand mixer, or steam oven or what either of them were, for that matter.

"What exactly does that song say?" she whispered, "That only a fool would rush in?"

She laughed at herself. That's exactly what it was. Foolishness. Foolish to feel the posters staring down at her. She wasn't rushing at all.

Still, she couldn't stop herself from finishing the first line of the beautiful, haunting song.

Her voice a husky whisper, she sang the words softly, as if it was a lullaby to the sleeping man.

Her voice fell into utter stillness.

And she recognized the truth of it. She was falling in love with him. Or maybe, more accurately, had never fallen out.

She had loved him as a girl. Oh, it had been an innocent love, based on his looks and his physique, and his charm, but still, that wild crush on him had been her first experience with love outside of her family. That night that he had walked into the gala, and she had tried to leave before he even saw her, hadn't she sensed the danger of him?

Hadn't some part of her known that despite the dating sites, despite going through the motions of wanting love, she hadn't really? She hadn't felt brave enough for it. Hadn't she known as soon as she'd laid eyes on him, he would be the one that would call it from her, that need to be brave, to engage love again, to risk its slings and arrows?

She gazed at him a little longer, and then turned rapidly on her heel, and nearly ran from the room and from his house, and from the hard hammering of her own heart.

Once home, Bree busied herself with laundry and the multitude of other things that had gotten stacked up while she had been trying to get her cookie orders caught up. She was also trying, unsuccessfully, to win back the affection of her neglected cat with his favorite game, but his chasing of the red light seemed desolate at best.

Her phone rang. She stared at the caller ID. There was that hammering in her heart again!

"Hello?" She hoped she didn't sound breathless.

"You sound out of breath. What am I getting you from?"

She tucked the laser pointer behind a plant, as if he could see it, as if it was evidence of a life that had gotten too staid, too safe.

"I was just coming up from the apartment-building laundry room with a basket," she said. Okay. Fifteen minutes ago. She was *not* still out of breath from that. "I take the stairs. My version of a StairMaster."

She was talking to a billionaire about basement-laundry facilities and stairs. He probably hadn't done his own laundry in years.

"You weren't supposed to let me fall asleep," Brand chided her. His voice was so natural, as if this was the most natural thing in the world, his calling her.

She felt something in her relax, just a bit. She thought of baking cookies with him, and the way his face had looked when he was sleeping.

Okay. He was a brilliant businessman. He was a billionaire. He was also still just Brand.

"I know you have your own formula for dealing with jet lag, but you just looked so tired. I didn't have the heart to wake you up."

"I have chocolate around my lips."

She giggled, even though she did not want to be thinking about his lips.

"I was thinking about what you said about taking a couple of days off," Brand said. "Are you going to spend them doing laundry?"

"Possibly," she said cautiously. She tried to think of something more exciting that she could tell him she was doing with her days off, but she was coming up blank. The sound of his voice was having that effect on her.

"Look, when I've been under a lot of stress, or I've been really busy—or if I'm fighting jet lag—I like to go kayaking. It grounds me."

"Oh," she said. Just when she was thinking she could dismiss his billionaire status, he had to show her the difference in their worlds. Basement laundry. Trying to get your cat to play. Jet lag. Kayaking.

"Have you ever done it?" he asked.

"No," she said, a little tightly.

"Would you like to?"

She had to sit down. Was Brand Wallace asking her on a date? And then it hit her. No, not a date.

More of the same. Poor girl. Had an affair. Ended up pregnant. Left school. Life in ruins. Needs looking after. Needs bolstering. It was so far from how she wanted him to feel that she could have screamed. Instead she bit down hard on her lip.

"Are you there?" he asked.

"Are you asking me because you feel sorry for me?" she finally asked.

"Yeah," he said, "I am."

She didn't know what to say to that. Well, besides no, she couldn't go on a date with him on that basis, because it wasn't really a date. She wasn't even sure what it was.

"There I was in Bali while you were slaving away over cookies. I've been thinking about your jailhouse pallor."

"Oh, brother," she said. She had been so far off

the mark it wasn't even funny. He wasn't thinking about her confidence at all. Well, maybe it was still a little funny. Or maybe not. Here she was thinking she was falling in love, and he was thinking about jailhouse pallor.

"It's making me feel guilty about the trip to Bali. I hate feeling guilty."

"I thought maybe you were asking me because you felt sorry for me," she said. "After I confided in you about what happened to me in college."

"Weird," he said.

"In what way?"

"That you would think I would perceive you as weak, because of that. The opposite is true. I find you very brave."

"Me?"

"Yes, you. You don't see yourself as brave?"

"No, not really." Bree had never, not even once, thought of herself as brave. Though she supposed maybe it did take a certain amount of bravery to wear that silly cookie beret and her quilted apron!

"That's how I see you," he said firmly. "It takes a lot of guts to start a business, especially after your dreams have pretty much had the crap kicked out of them. You picked yourself up, you dusted yourself off, you started again."

So, he had heard everything she had said to him, and instead of making him see her as weak and foolish, a girl who had let her heart get her in a world of trouble, he saw it in a completely different light.

"You have what it takes, Bree, you have what it takes to make your business whatever you want it to be."

"Thanks."

"But you have to take care of yourself, too. You have to know how to intersperse hard work with fun and time away from your business."

So, it wasn't really a date then. More like a mentorship. She should say no, shouldn't she? Just on principle? Just because, in their minds, it was obvious they were moving the relationship in different directions?

"Hey, I don't ask just anybody to go sea kayaking. It's not for the faint of heart."

Another very good reason to say no. She was

not sure Brand had mentioned the *sea* part of kayaking when he had first mentioned it. Kayaks were very small boats, weren't they? In a sea that could roil up, cold and dangerous, in a second? In channels shared with huge ships and creatures of the deep?

"In fact," Brand said, "I've never asked anyone to go with me before."

"You haven't?"

"It's kind of my sanctuary out there. A deep and private pleasure. But also, amazing stress relief. Which is why I'm asking you. I know you've been under enormous stress, with the fire, and catching up on those orders."

Bree listened to what he wasn't saying.

It struck her that, despite the "mentorship" spin on this, he was nervous about asking her. She was almost positive about that: the gorgeous, self-confident, successful Brand Wallace was nervous about asking her to do something with him.

Suddenly, the whole "unknown" of it, the adventure of it—not just of sea kayaking, but of getting to know Brand better—was completely irresistible.

Something had been healed in her when she told him her most completely guarded secrets, when her tears had fallen like a secret ingredient into those cookies.

And this is what it was: for a long time, despite going through the motions, despite going on the dating sites, despite saying something different, she had been saying no to life instead of yes.

And suddenly she just wanted to say yes, even though it sounded faintly terrifying. But she wanted to be brave again, even if it ended in heartache, to embrace whatever life, in all its magnificence, offered her.

More, she wanted to trust someone again.

None of which she said to him. To Brand, as casually as she could, as if a billionaire invited her to go kayaking with him every day, Bree said, "That sounds fun. Sure."

CHAPTER ELEVEN

BREE HAD TO look up online what to wear for kayaking and it was only then that she realized she knew nothing about what she had let herself in for. Was she going to be paddling her own kayak? She hoped not! Most sites recommended a few lessons before you went out on your own, particularly so you would know what to do if you capsized.

Capsized? In ocean water in May? She checked what the temperature of the water would be. Forty-six degrees Fahrenheit. Not a death sentence, but still, even if you were wearing the recommended clothing it would be simply awful. Wouldn't it? Unless Brand saved her…

Given her investment in the cloak, she couldn't really justify buying an outfit made specifically for kayaking, so she was pleased with the look she managed to assemble: cotton leggings, a T-shirt topped with an oversize wool sweater and a light jacket.

Brand was already at the English Bay parking lot they had agreed to meet at when she got there. He was single-handedly sliding a slender kayak from the roof rack of the vehicle.

Bree paused for a moment, just watching him, the play of muscle, the ease with which he handled himself, before she got out of her vehicle. He was gorgeous and rugged-looking in multi-pocketed outdoor pants and a hooded jacket.

As she approached him, she was welcomed with a smile that made her feel like her heart was a flower opening up to the sun after a long rain.

After they greeted each other, she studied the kayak.

"It has two holes in it," she noted. "I thought you said you usually go by yourself?"

He slid her a look. "I didn't figure you for the jealous type."

"It's dating the Elvis guy," she admitted. "It's given me a suspicious mind."

He threw back his head and laughed. She knew, with sudden delight, it was going to be that kind of day—laughter-filled and fun. His laughter was a sound that eased some of the nervousness in her, caused both by trying something new and more one-on-one time with the billionaire.

"By myself is relative, I guess," Brand said, answering her question. "Beau usually takes the front hole, which, by the way, is generally referred to as a cockpit."

The idea of that big dog in the kayak with him made her laugh, too. She'd been nervous, but now with the sun on her face, and the smell of the sea in the air, and Brand smiling at her, and handling the kayak with easy strength, she could feel her confidence rising.

He took her cell phone and keys and put them in a waterproof bag.

"We aren't going to get wet, are we?" she said, and her confidence dipped a little.

"It's Vancouver. It could start raining anytime."

"I didn't mean that."

"I know you didn't. I am seriously hoping we

are not going to get wet. But we'll put these on just in case."

Bree was glad she had not purchased an expensive outfit when he handed her an ugly yellow life vest, which made about as much fashion statement as wearing a neon marshmallow!

He came and helped her when her zipper stuck.

"Is this Beau's, too?" she said, blinking up at him as he leaned in close to her to unstick the zipper.

"Believe me, you'd smell it if it was."

And they were laughing again, even as she became aware that what she smelled was him: a delicious scent, deeply masculine, outdoorsy, clean.

He picked up the kayak and swung it up over his head, part of it resting on his back.

"I can help," she offered.

"Don't worry. I'm used to doing it by myself." She took the paddles and followed him down to the water's edge, admiring his strength and the broadness of his shoulders, the ease of long practice that made what he was doing seem natural to him.

He set down the kayak and pushed it into the water, but just a bit.

"Okay, get in. Straddle it, feet on both sides, paddle in the middle, push it along until you can step in to that front cockpit."

Before she knew it, she was in the kayak, and she hadn't even gotten her feet wet, though she had worn light canvas sneakers just in case. When she wiggled a bit to get comfortable, the kayak rocked, despite him steadying the back of it.

But then he shoved it hard, and got in the back cockpit in one easy motion. The vessel seemed to stabilize with his weight, and they glided off the beach.

"We'll do a fairly short paddle today," he said, "Just to get you used of it."

He was saying that as if there might be more excursions!

"Don't feel like you have to paddle with me. Rest if you start getting tired. And don't be shy to tell me if you've had enough."

And then he went over some of the rudiments of steering and paddling together. They practiced stopping, turning and reversing direction a few times. It was fun! She hated to admit how right he had been about her life not having enough fun in it.

Maybe this wasn't a date. She wasn't quite sure about how to define this outing, but whatever it was it was so much better than anything that had ever happened on e-Us. Going for coffee suddenly seemed like the most ridiculous way to get to know a person! And meeting someone at the bookstore hardly seemed better.

Because this was getting to know a person: learning to paddle together, watching in awe as eagles soared and fish jumped, laughing when she accidentally splashed him and then laughing harder when she did it again on purpose.

The setting was glorious and kayaking seemed very simple, but she suspected he was doing most of the work. Before she knew it, they were gliding effortlessly through the stillness of the dark water toward the mouth of the bay.

Tell him when she had had enough? Really, it felt as if she could never get enough of this.

It occurred to her, once they were way out in the water, that she had him exactly where she wanted him.

Because she could finally ask him questions he could not get away from. She could, maybe, find out where all this was going. Was this a date? Was this delightful little outing going to lead to something else?

Don't be terrifying, Bree warned herself. *No wedding bells or babies.*

They paused to rest off the shore by Stanley Park. She was breathing hard, and her arms and shoulders ached, but in the nicest way. Not too far off was the hum of traffic, and she could see people walking and biking the Seawall, but she had a sense of it being deeply quiet. The kayak rocked ever so gently on the sea. He passed her a bottle of water.

"Do you like it?" he asked. "Kayaking?"

"Love it." She took a deep sip of her water. "Brand, why don't you have friends who are, um, women?"

He took a sudden interest in something on the shoreline. "Is that a deer?"

She squinted where he was pointing. "I think it's a branch."

"Oh."

"How come?" she said, refusing to be distracted. She might never have him in a boat again!

"What makes you think I don't?" he said, raising an eyebrow at her.

"Your house told me."

"What? How?"

"A million ways. No forgotten umbrella. No makeup around. No *The Lucky One* or *Dirty Dancing* or *The Notebook* in your movie collection."

"Did you go in my bedroom?"

"Of course not! I didn't have to to know you basically live out of three rooms. I bet your bedroom is a man cave, too."

"You're right," he said with a shrug. "The house is a masculine haven inhabited by Beau and me."

"I'm trying to get the *why* no significant other." *When you're obviously so irresistible.*

"I'm busy," he said uncomfortably.

She waited, not commenting. As she had hoped, there was no place to run from the question.

"I had a girlfriend. We saw each other for two years. We weren't engaged, though I think she wanted to be. We actually, ah, tried living together. She moved in. And she moved out again. Three days later."

"What happened?" she asked in horror. Three days? Was something horribly wrong with him? Three days?

"Beau."

"What?"

"He ate some of her stuff. Like her sofa. She gave me an ultimatum. Dog or me."

She knew she shouldn't laugh. She knew she shouldn't. But she giggled. "She knew you had a dog, obviously, before she moved in."

"Yeah, she just hadn't had to live with him before."

"Fantasy meets reality?" She would do well to remember this. He was the kind of man a woman might build a fantasy around.

But for two years? His ex hadn't known after two years how much that dog meant to him? She could actually say to him "dog or me" and think she was going to win that one?

Bree felt she knew Brand better than that after just this tiny bit of time!

"She took down the Elvis posters. She didn't even ask."

"Actually, since you mention it, I'm curious about the Elvis thing. I don't get the impression you like Elvis much."

"Actually, I know it really wasn't about Beau or the Elvis posters," he said carefully.

She was looking over her shoulder at him. Unless she was mistaken, he was deliberately not telling her how he felt about Elvis. He had the cookie jar, yes, and the posters, but when she had put on Elvis music that morning he had arrived home from Bali, she was almost positive he had flinched.

"So what's it really about then?"

"I'm not cut out for it. The whole domestic-bliss thing. I wanted to be, but I'm not. We'd been dating two years. It was fine when we both had our own spaces, but as soon as she moved in I felt suffocated by her. A two-year relationship in ruins, and I was so happy to see her marching out of my house, I was practically dancing. I don't know what that says about me."

"That she wasn't the right woman?" Bree suggested mildly.

"I don't think that's it. I think it's more that I'm not the right guy. Maybe I'm just like my old man. No staying power. When the fun stops, I'm gone."

This brutal self-assessment surprised her so much it put her off the trail of how he really felt about Elvis.

"I don't believe that," she said firmly. "I've seen how you treat people. Not just me, but your employees. Chelsea told me your lawyer who called her has hired his own fire investigator. She's practically a stranger to you, and you did that for her. You're a good, good man, Brand Wallace."

"Aw, shucks," he said with mild sarcasm, clearly trying to brush off the compliment.

"No, I mean it."

"Does this mean you've forgiven me for not kissing you at your senior prom?"

"That was part of being a good man, wasn't it?"

"Yeah, I guess."

"I think we should have a do-over."

"What?"

She could not believe this was her, but one thing she was learning was you only came this way once. Why not take chances? Why not go after what you wanted? Why not take a risk?

She was falling in love with him. She knew that. Even today, it felt as if it was deepening around them. The level of comfort, of connection, of companionship.

And something was definitely brewing on a deeper level, too.

Awareness.

A wanting.

To taste him again. To know him in a different way.

In a way, his choosing kayaking was the safest thing he could have done. There was a whole boat in between them! No cuddling was possible. No physical contact. The closest she could come to touching him was splashing him!

Was she just going to let him relegate her to friend-I-can-decompress-with position? Was she constantly going to be the one *helped*? No, for once in her life she was taking a chance. She was going to put it all on the line.

"Your company's charity ball is coming up," she said.

"Did the organizer get in touch? Are you making cookies for it?"

"Yes, for the midnight lunch, plus four-cookie boxes for party favors, though that's not why I mentioned it."

He waited. She glanced over his shoulder at him.

She took a deep breath. "I'd like to go."

He dipped his paddle in, setting them in motion, trying to move away from it. "Of course you are welcome to go!"

"Not as the cookie caterer."

The strength of his stroke carried them a long ways out into the stillness of the water.

"With you," she told him firmly.

She could feel the bravery in her. She could feel a shift in her perception. She wasn't the hapless, heartbroken woman pleading for people to choose her on the internet, desperate for a first date, never mind a second one.

She just wasn't that person anymore. Maybe just speaking about what had happened to her with Brand had clarified something in her.

Helped her make a vow.

No more being a victim. Not of men. Not of life. Not of circumstances.

She was going to take the helm. She was going to steer. She was going to move in the direction she wanted to, not wait for someone else to move her. Instead of waiting passively for something to happen, she was going to take charge of her own life,

She wasn't waiting, hope-filled, for something to happen to her. She was making it happen.

He didn't answer. His paddle entered the water and pulled the kayak forward with such force

Bree wondered if she had ever been helping paddle at all. He looked wary of her invitation.

As well he should, she thought happily, as well he should! Because she was changing right before his eyes. It might not have hit him yet, but what she was really asking him was did he want to explore what was going on between them in a new way? Did he want to move forward?

Yes or no.

As simple as that.

But, of course, she should know by now, nothing in her life was ever simple. Because as that question hung there in the air between them, as she explored the meaning of bravery in this brand-new and infinitely exciting way, out of the corner of her eye, she caught a movement.

She swung her head toward the ripple in the water maybe a hundred feet to the left of the bow of the kayak.

The ripple became larger. A huge round back, black and shiny as a freshly tarred road, rose out of the water.

Her heart felt as if it might beat out of her chest.

A mountain was shoving its way out of the gray endlessness of the ocean, way, way too close to them. The powerful movement was rocking the kayak. They were in very real danger of being capsized by a whale!

CHAPTER TWELVE

THE KILLER WHALE swam beside them, its ripples rocking the small kayak. Thankfully, it quickly outdistanced them. It blew out its top spout, a geyser of water droplets making a rainbow in the air. And then the whale's terrific bulk lifted out of the water. The grace, in a creature so large, was astounding. It shot up in the air, a cork released from a bottle. And then it crashed back down with such force that they were sprayed with water, and the kayak rocked more violently, before settling into stillness.

Brand had never seen a whale that close, not in all his years of being on the water.

Bree turned and looked at him. When the whale had first begun to surface, she had gone dead quiet and utterly still. He had been able to read the tension in her posture.

But now, all of that was gone. She was radiant as she turned her wide eyes to him.

"Oh!" she breathed. "Oh! That was the most amazing thing I have ever experienced."

His male ego wanted to remind her that she had just kissed him, only days ago. Certainly for him that kiss had been as earth-rocking as the breaching of the whale.

The whale had distracted her from her invitation to him. On the surface, it seemed as if maybe she was asking him to go to the charity ball. With him.

But, of course, with her, there was another layer to it.

Bree was asking him to define what was going on between them. He'd known, as soon as he had to escape to Bali to get away from her pull, what it was.

He was in the danger zone.

And maybe it was already too late to fix that, to escape it, to change it to something else.

The way she was looking at him now, her face

so radiant, a person so capable of wonder, after all that had happened to her, it asked him about the nature of bravery.

It asked him if he could be a better man.

It asked him if he could stand the loneliness of going back to a life that didn't have her in it.

He was not a man used to being terrified, and yet really, he was aware that had been there since the moment he had rescued her from under that cascade of her own cookies at the Stars Come Out at Night gala.

That she would ask more of him. That she would require more of him than anyone had ever required before.

That she would hold out to him the most enticing gift of all: an ability to hope for things he had given up on a long time ago.

There was a possibility he was constitutionally unsuited to the world he saw shining in her eyes like a beacon calling a weary soldier home.

But he had warned her of that. He had tried to tell her.

And this was what she was trying to tell him: she was not the innocent girl he'd escorted to her prom any longer.

She was a woman, capable of making her own choices, capable of embracing all the risks of the unknown.

Love. The greatest unknown of all.

Love, that capricious vixen who called you in, then shattered you on the rocks.

Somehow, he could not see being shattered on the rocks with Bree. Her eyes were warm, everything about her was genuine.

She wasn't going to hurt him.

And so he said, "Sure, let's go to my charity ball together."

He said it casually, as if it was not every bit as thrilling and as terrifying as that whale breaching the water beside them had been. Saying it was a lift of his shoulder that said "no big deal," as if he had not just stepped off a cliff, and was waiting to see if the parachute would open.

And the parachute was her.

* * *

Despite a paddle against a slight current coming back in to English Bay, Bree was brimming over with energy. Life felt the way it had not felt in so long.

Exciting and ripe with potential.

"I'm famished," she said, when they had pulled the kayak up the beach and hoisted it onto his roof rack. "Should we go grab a bite?"

This was the new bold her! Taking chances. Asking Brand to spend yet more time with her. He was going to say—

"Sure. What did you have in mind?"

"I love that Hot Diggity food truck."

"Hot Diggity?"

"Hot dogs. If you give me back my phone, I'll check their schedule and see where they are today."

He was smirking as he handed her the phone. "You know, I can afford a little better than a hot dog."

"You probably can. I'm buying."

"No, you're not."

"Look, Brand, if it's going to be a relationship of equals, you have to let me do my bit, too."

The word *relationship* word wavered in the air between them, like a wave of heat shimmering off hot pavement.

"Did you actually get stiffed for the coffee with the e-Us loser, or did you offer to buy it?" he asked.

"Different lifetime," she said, scrolling through her phone. "I've moved on. You should, too. He's on Robson Street today, by the art gallery."

"The guy who stiffed you for coffee?" Brand asked, surprised.

She glanced at him and saw he was teasing her. Warmth unfurled in her like a flag. "Parking won't be fun."

"My office has some spots down there, if you don't object to that on some principle of equality. We could travel together."

She certainly wasn't going to object to that part.

And so Bree found herself in the deep and luxurious leather passenger seat, enjoying his confidence as he maneuvered his oversize vehicle through downtown traffic. He turned on his CD player. No Elvis. Light classical.

He parked in a private stall in a private lot and they walked the short distance to Hot Diggity. He didn't put up too much of a fight about letting her pay, and just as she had hoped, he fell in love with the hot dogs.

By the time he drove her back out to English Bay, the sun was setting, and both conversation and silence felt comfortable between them. He had an old blanket in the car, and they sat together on it, shoulders touching, until there was no light left.

"My turn to supply food tomorrow night," he said as he walked her to her car. "Meet me at my office around six?"

"Okay."

For a moment he hesitated. For a moment she hesitated.

And then his arms were around her, and he pulled her into him, kissed her soundly on the lips and let her go. They stood there, studying each other with a kind of wonder.

"I don't remember when I've had such a perfect day," she confessed.

"I don't know when I have, either."

"Are you scared?" she asked softly.

"Terrified," he answered.

"Me, too."

"The good kind of terrified, like when a very large whale breaches beside a very small vessel."

And then he kissed her again, harder this time. "Get in your car," he said huskily, "before I invite you home with me. And it wouldn't be to make cookies."

She got in her car. She felt so intoxicated with lust she didn't know how she would drive. Somehow she managed to get home. And somehow she managed to get through the next day until it was time to be at his office.

It was much emptier than the last time she had seen it, but just the same, Beau came barreling through the door. This time she wasn't so shocked to see him. In fact, she felt delighted. And glad she had opted for slender-fitting jeans that could stand up to him. The rose-colored silk blouse, however, didn't fare so well!

Brand came through the door. "Beau! I don't know what it is about him and you. He managed to give me the slip and was through that door before I knew you'd arrived."

"What did you have planned for dinner? Do I have to change?" she asked.

Brand's eyes moved to the wet splotch on her breast. "Uh—"

"That's a yes."

"Well, we're eating in."

"Here?" she said, surprised.

"Yeah, I thought we'd have dinner and then I'd show you the climbing wall. And the ball pit."

She giggled.

"I have extra shirts here."

"Why not?" she said.

His office was dark, except for candles that burned on the coffee table between the love seats.

As the sun went down, the Vancouver skyline was lighting up outside his windows.

She could see the table had been set. And that food was already there. For a guy who claimed to be hopeless at relationships, he seemed to be doing just fine at romance!

"Here," he said. He went into a large cabinet that turned out to be a wardrobe and passed her a shirt. "Powder room is through there."

The powder room was exquisite and luxurious. She put on the men's shirt. It was clean and crisp, way too large, and for some absurd reason it made her feel sexier than hell.

She came out, his shirt to her knees, with her own soiled shirt balled up in her hand.

"Give that to me. I'll put it in the basket that gets sent out to the cleaners."

"Don't be sil—"

He gave her a look. She passed him her blouse.

"In any other context, me getting you out of your blouse might be kind of fun." He raised that delightfully wicked eyebrow. Then her smile died.

She had the feeling he found her as sexy in his shirt as she felt!

"Have a seat," he said. "I took the liberty of ordering from one of my favorite places."

He poured her a glass of wine, and she looked at the plate before her. It held a salad, and she took her fork and took a tentative taste. The salad had greens, but also tomatoes, avocado and crab. It was exquisite, of course!

"Well?" he asked.

It was so endearing that he was anxious that she be pleased. Really, it was like something out of a dream.

"It's not Hot Diggity," she said thoughtfully, "but it's passably good. The bouquet of the balsamic vinegar is lovely."

And then they were laughing together, and as always, when they laughed together everything else fell away.

The rest of the menu was just as exquisite as the salad, as they dined on grilled quail, served with tiny roasted potatoes, and fresh green beans in a lime butter sauce.

"This is so good," Bree said.

"This is what happens when a man doesn't use his own kitchen," Brand told her. "He figures out where to get the best takeout in the city."

The dog, who had been sitting quietly, moaned softly.

"He knows we're done. I won't let him beg at the table, but I always give him a little something after."

Brand opened a bag from the same restaurant, removed a container and went over to a huge bowl.

"What's he getting?" Bree said as she came over and stood beside him.

"Same thing as us. Deboned."

For a moment, she felt extremely awkward and out of place. She was with a man who thought nothing of feeding his dog deboned quail from one of Vancouver's finest restaurants.

He turned back to her. "You want dessert now? Or do you want to try the climbing wall?"

"Definitely the climbing wall!"

There seemed to be no other people in the office tonight, and they had the "play" equipment to themselves. Beau came with them, and Brand threw one of his toys in the ball pit. The big dog leaped in and soon balls were flying everywhere as he searched joyously for his toy.

The awkwardness was gone, just like that. Brand knew how to have fun!

He helped her strap on a harness, and gave her a few tips for her first attempt at the wall. He put on his own harness, though it was obvious he did not need one. With the confidence and agility of a billy goat he topped the wall in about twenty seconds. From his perch up there, he called tips down to her.

"Oh," she cried as, just when she thought she had gotten the hang of it, she fell. But the harness took her weight easily. He was beside her in a second, showing her how to get back onto the wall, or lower herself to the floor and start again. She lost her hold several times, which was good, because she also totally lost her fear. The harness caught her and swung her gently each time.

They spent the rest of the evening finding different ways up the wall. Like the kayaking, it proved to be a terrific way to get to know each other. It involved communication, but not that interview-style intensity that Brand had pointed out was a flaw of the online dating world.

Beau finally captured his toy and abandoned the pit to go chew on it.

Since muscles she did not even know she had were aching, Bree was glad when Brand suggested they take over the pit. Following his example, she let herself fall in over the side, arms spread wide. The balls caught her and cushioned her, and she shrieked with delight, just lying there. Brand swam the backstroke and then dove into the colorful sea of balls. Bree joined him, until she was laughing so hard her stomach ached from it.

They retreated back to his office and had coffee and crème brûlée for dessert.

And then he walked her home, through quiet Vancouver streets, one hand in hers and the other holding Beau's leash.

Bree felt so happy. She thought they probably

looked just like one of those couples she had always envied, out with their dog on an evening walk.

He insisted on seeing her right to her apartment door.

"I'd invite you in," she said, "but I don't think Oliver is ready to meet Beau."

"I'm sure he's quite jealous of all the time you've spent away. And now, after arriving with the scent of a strange dog on you, the slathering beast is right on his doorstep."

"I'm not worried. Oliver's forgiveness can be purchased with a new toy," Bree said, and pulled a bright purple mouse from her purse. "Voilà!"

They both laughed when Beau made a try for the toy.

"Plus, Oliver has selected my neighbor as a suitable slave in my absence. She spoils him atrociously. She's recently lost her husband, and I think she and the cat are both loving the relationship."

Of course, Oliver was not ready to meet Beau, but really that was just a convenient excuse not to invite Brand in. It wasn't the real reason, and she suspected he knew it, too. There was something lovely unfolding between them. It felt new and fragile. To move things to a physical plane too soon would bring a layer of complication to what was going on between them that she knew she was not ready for.

He seemed to feel the same way. He kissed her on the lips. It was a beautiful kiss. Welcoming and tender. Brand seemed to recognize exactly where she was at, because he pulled away and looked at her with a kind of respect and reverence that she had never experienced before.

"I usually take Beau for a really long walk in the morning," he said. "Are you game?"

"Absolutely."

And so they began to tangle their lives together in lovely ways: walking the dog, grabbing a bite to eat, watching a movie at his place, cooking dinner at hers. One memorable afternoon, they opened the Klingon-dictionary app on her phone, and they sat out in his backyard in the spring sunshine trying out phrases until they were both rolling on the ground laughing, with Beau leaping joyously between them.

A commercial kitchen space opened up for her, and she moved out of his kitchen. In a way she was sad to be leaving it, because it was so beautiful and she had felt so at home there, but in a way she was happy that their business interests were separating.

They did such ordinary things, but they did things that reflected his wealth and status as well. He took her on a helicopter tour of Vancouver, he rented a yacht for a day, complete with a chef, and he flew them on a private jet one night for a play in San Francisco, where they met Bree's mother and her husband.

It was a beautiful evening.

Her mother looked at her, when they had a moment alone together in the theater powder room, and hugged her hard.

"I know you thought I moved on too quickly from your dad," she said. "But when you love someone the way I loved him, the thought of not having love in your life is unbearable. Of course, every love is different. What Mike and I have is not the same as what your father and I shared. And yet, it is lovely, too. So lovely."

And then she added softly, "But you know that now, don't you, my dear Bree? That a life without love is unbearable?"

Bree thought, just as her mother, she had probably known that all along. Life without love was unbearable. It had made her such easy prey for a bad person. And then it had made her back off of love altogether.

But her mother was so right, that life without love was like crossing an endless desert, thirsty for water you could not find.

Her mother confirmed what Bree already knew in her heart. She was not going down that road again. She felt like a completely different person than the girl she had been before.

"Brand is such a good man," her mother said. "Your father always knew that about him. I have a feeling he'd be extraordinarily pleased right now."

But, for all that, for all that Bree got to experience lifestyles of the rich and famous, it seemed to be the small and ordinary things that had taken on a shine, that made Bree feel alive and engaged and as if happiness was a ball of light in her stomach that glowed ever more strongly outward.

Everyone noticed it. Her clients, Chelsea, her neighbors, her girlfriends.

When Brand went away on business trips, she stayed at his place and looked after Beau, who had completely stolen her heart. Oliver began to come along, and soon ruled Beau with an iron paw.

Brand would always bring her back small, enchanting gifts—a crystal butterfly from Sweden, an exquisite wooden carving from Thailand, a soapstone polar bear from the Canadian north. They even had a tradition: as soon as he came home, they baked cookies together, sometimes in her tiny apartment kitchen, sometimes in his state-of-the-art kitchen.

By the time of the charity ball, they had been seeing each other for a month. Bree was certain of how she felt. She was certain it was not an infatuation, certain where she wanted it to go, certain of Brand's place in her future.

Everything she had known the night she had heard that song in her head—"Can't Help Falling in Love"—was confirmed.

And so Bree decided to find a dress for that charity ball that would tell him all that as much as words ever could.

That would tell him beyond a shadow of a doubt that she was ready for whatever came next.

CHAPTER THIRTEEN

"I CAN'T FIND the right dress," Bree wailed to Chelsea a week later as they were locking up the new kitchen for the day. "Time's running out. I can't go to Brand's charity ball looking like the very same person I was at my high-school prom. And yet everything I've tried on does exactly that. It makes me feel as if I'm a kid pretending to be a grown-up."

"We could remake one of my salsa costumes," Chelsea said. "It would be easy."

Bree had attended a number of Chelsea's dance competitions. She made all her own outfits. "Chelsea, I don't know. Your outfits are gorgeous, but kind of over-the-top sexy."

"You just said you wanted to be sexy."

"Yes, but—"

"I have a red one. Red always makes men sit up

and take notice. It's short, but I could add some layers to it. We're almost the same size. I think it would look phenomenal on you. Come home with me right now, we'll try it. You have nothing to lose."

That was true. She had nothing to lose. It was not as if she had found the right dress anywhere else. Plus, the price was right.

Chelsea lived in a cute little basement suite not very far from the new kitchen. It was an easy walk, and they went in.

Bree stopped. There was a large pair of men's sneakers at the door.

"Oh," Chelsea said with a blush, "Reed left those here."

"Reed?" Bree asked. She looked at her young assistant closely. She had been so wrapped up in herself that she hadn't notice a different kind of sparkle about Chelsea. Who was now blushing pink.

"He's the fire investigator our side hired."

Meaning the one *Brand* had hired.

"Don't look at me like that. Of course, he can't

get involved with me while he's doing an investigation."

Which, of course, begged the question, why his shoes would be there, but Chelsea looked so pretty and so flustered that Bree didn't have the heart to pursue it.

Chelsea, eager to change the subject, brought out the dress, still in its dry-cleaning wrapper.

Bree took off the wrapper. The dress slid into her hands, surprisingly cool, since it looked so hot, like flames.

"Put it on," Chelsea insisted, and Bree went through to her tiny bathroom.

"No underwear," Chelsea shouted.

Good grief! Still, Bree put the dress on, then turned to face herself in the full-length mirror on the back of the door.

"Cripes," she said, astounded.

The dress fit her like a glove. The top was pure red, with tiny spaghetti straps at the shoulders. The neckline plunged to a narrow waist, where it took on the color of flame, leaf-like layers of fabric in colors of orange and yellow and several shades of red.

"Come out," Chelsea said.

"I'm scared to," Bree answered back, but then opened the door and stepped out. Chelsea's eyes widened.

"It's all wrong," Bree said at the very same time Chelsea said, "It's so right."

"It's too short."

"I knew that. But I've got lots of that fabric, and an idea how I can make it floor-length."

"And the neckline is too—"

"Shush. One little stitch. Here, I'll get a pin and show you."

That single pin changed everything.

And then Chelsea was at her feet, pinning and tucking and pinning some more. "This is just to give you an idea. It will be way more sophisticated. Fall leaves, until you move, and then each piece of fabric will move differently and catch the light differently. It will change from fall leaves to flame."

Finally, Chelsea was satisfied and told Bree she

could go back into the bathroom, the location of the only full-length mirror in her tiny apartment.

Bree was almost afraid to look. She turned to the mirror with her eyes closed. Slowly, she opened them, and when she did, her heart beat double time. The dress was incredible, with its beautiful silk leaves falling to the floor, dancing around her. Just as Chelsea had promised, when she moved, the light caught the fabric and turned it to flame.

Chelsea managed to squeeze through the door to join Bree. "These outfits are made to celebrate the female form," she said, "and to move all on their own. It's really a seduction."

A seduction? Bree gulped. Was she ready for that?

She realized it wasn't Brand who had looked at her like a child pretending to be an adult, but that that was the role she had cast herself in.

And suddenly she felt so completely adult, she could feel herself stepping over some imaginary line that separated a girl from a woman.

Oh, yeah, she felt so ready for that! These

weeks of keeping each other at arm's length, of only sharing chaste kisses, the longing building to something almost unbearable…

Chelsea moved in behind her and scooped up her hair. It made Bree's neck look long and elegant, and her eyes look huge, dark and startled, like those of a doe.

"I don't know how I can thank you," Bree said.

"Oh, Bree, you already have. You have had faith in me in the face of evidence you should not have. I know you think there's a possibility I set the kitchen on fire. Thank you for not suing me."

"That's ridiculous. The suing part."

"But not the catching-the-kitchen-on-fire part?" Chelsea said with wry self-recognition. And then they were laughing, and Bree felt as if she had been given many gifts.

A man she loved, and the sister she never had.

"It will be ready before the ball," Chelsea promised. "And you will be the most ravishing woman Mr. Brand Wallace has ever laid eyes on."

Bree slipped out of the dress and came back

into the main area in her ordinary-girl clothes. But Chelsea wasn't finished with her yet.

"I'm just going to show you a few moves," she said. "Subtle, but sexy as hell."

Bree's eyes got very wide as Chelsea demonstrated exactly what she meant!

The night of the ball arrived and if Bree had had another outfit suitable to go change into before Brand arrived, she probably would have. She felt nervous and naked. Who did she think she was? she wondered. Julia Roberts?

She, indeed, looked like a movie star—red-carpet ready, which was, as Chelsea had assured her, a very good thing.

Tonight was as close as Vancouver got to a red-carpet event!

But as soon as Bree opened the door, and saw the look on Brand's face, she was happy—almost deliriously so—that she had not lost her nerve about the dress.

Because Brand looked like a man slain. His mouth fell open, and his eyes darkened with heady desire and drank her in with a kind of thirst that could never be quenched.

"You look absolutely stunning," he said, his voice hoarse.

He reached for her and kissed her on the cheek, put her away from himself and stared. "It seems not so long ago you were telling me how ordinary you were," he said.

She realized, with a shiver of pure appreciation, this was true. Being with him, feeling cherished by him, had made her feel beautiful and confident in a way she never, ever had before. He took her hand and walked her outside her building.

A long, sleek, white limo waited, the uniformed driver holding open the door for them. He tipped his hat to her, and called her "Miss."

Sinking into the luxurious leather and having Brand pour her some champagne into a flute was the beginning of a night out of a fairy tale. She floated through every minute of it. The entrance, chatting with people, nursing a drink and, finally, what she had been waiting for her whole life.

The thing she had got the tiniest taste of the

night of her prom, a taste that had left her wanting. She danced with Brand.

Not as a child, dancing with the man who had been talked into escorting her to her prom.

But as a woman who knew exactly what she wanted. It was an evening out of a dream. His eyes never left her. Every move he made was subtly sensual, welcoming her in a different way. Brand was so comfortable with himself, and with his body, and it made her more comfortable with her own newfound sexy side.

She demonstrated some of the moves Chelsea had shown her. They had exactly the right effect on him, making his eyes darken and his hands linger on the curves of her back and hip.

They laughed. They teased each other. They danced and their hands touched each other, as if they could not get enough.

Despite the fact there were so many beautiful people there, in gorgeous clothes and jewelry, moving in amazing ways, it felt as if the ballroom belonged to them and them alone. Their eyes rarely left each other. Even when they spoke to other people, it was as if they were in a bubble that really held only them.

Bree had that first glass of champagne, and then one more, not enough to be making her feel as intoxicated as she did.

The evening went both too quickly and too slowly, because she was anticipating the moment they were alone.

So, here they were, seemingly only a breath after he had picked her up, facing the last dance of the evening.

Bree was stunned when she heard the opening notes of the Elvis song "Can't Help Falling in Love." Had he requested it? She didn't think so.

It was the universe conspiring.

His hand found the small of her back and he pulled him in to her. They might have been the only two people in the room.

She put her head back so that she could look up into his beautiful face, so beloved to her now.

The last bars of the song melted over top of them and then the music ended, but what was flowing between them did not. He lowered his head. He took her lips. She reached up, almost on tiptoes, and returned his kiss. It was as if they were in the room alone together.

The heat was scorching.

"Do you mind taking a miss on the midnight buffet?" he whispered in her ear.

"No," she said, trembling.

His hand found the small of her back. Nodding here and there, he propelled her through the crowd. Suddenly they were out on a wet street, the rain refreshingly cool on her scorching skin.

And then they were in the back of the limo.

He stared straight ahead. So did she. She knew if they even glanced at one another, the chauffer was going to get much more of a show than he'd bargained for.

They tumbled out of the limo when it stopped at her apartment, almost running to the building's entrance. To a passerby it might have seemed they did not want to get wet.

But there was urgency between them now. To open the last chapter, to go to the place between them that had not yet been mapped.

That exquisite new country of pure discovery.

"Security cameras?" he whispered in the elevator.

"No."

He was on her. He had her backed against the wall of the elevator, his hands around her back, crushing her to him, her hands twined around his neck, pulling his lips to her own.

By the time the elevator door opened, they were both gasping with need, with red-hot desire. They tumbled from the elevator. Thank God, at this time of night, her hallway was abandoned.

With great effort, nearly dumping the contents of her tiny evening bag on the floor, she found her key. Her hands were shaking so badly she could not make the lock work.

He reached by her and took the key, inserted and twisted it.

The door fell open.

She stared at him.

He stared at her.

"Are you sure?" he growled.

"Yes," she whispered, and then stronger, because she had never been more sure of anything, she repeated, "Yes!"

CHAPTER FOURTEEN

THEY WERE IN the kitchen, their coats wet puddles of fabric on the floor. He lifted her onto the counter and, with her legs wrapped around him, she tasted him as if she could never get enough. Hungry. Starving.

All grown up. So filled with passion she was trembling with it. She could feel him trembling, too. He rubbed his whisker-roughened cheek down the delicate skin of her neck, as her nails dug into the broadness of his back.

His lips found hers again, no gentleness in them now, no tenderness.

He was a warrior conquering, he was taking what he wanted. But she was no captive, except maybe of her own heart's longings, because she met his savage taking of her lips with an answer of her own that was bold and uninhibited.

The woman in her explored the man in him—she tasted it, and touched it, and rode the enormous energy of it. It sizzled and hissed between them like a fire out of control. She was pulled toward the heat of it, helpless as a moth to a flame, sure to be scorched and yet unable to move away from what was happening between them.

His hands went to her hair. It tumbled out of its knot and scattered wildly around her shoulders. He kissed the low-cut space in her dress, between her breasts, and she moaned with desire, lifted his questing lips to her own and took them again.

And then a sound.

An insistent sound.

The quacking of a duck.

Stunned, she realized it was coming from him. She realized it was some kind of ringtone. Bree was even more stunned when Brand took his phone out of his pocket and answered it.

Bree had never heard that ringtone come from his phone before. In fact, he rarely answered or looked at his phone when they were together.

But now he took it, his features set in grim

lines. He held up a finger to her, answered and went out the door of her apartment.

He came back in seconds later. “I’m sorry,” he said, running a hand through his hair. “I’ve got an emergency. I have to leave.”

“An emergency?” she whispered, feeling shattered by her own longing, by the fact what was happening between them had not been so sacred that the phone could be ignored.

“An urgent family matter.”

She stared at him, trying to figure out the incongruity of using a quack tone for an emergency. And yet, there was no doubting the gravity of the situation. His face, so familiar to her, was completely closed, set in the ferocious, impenetrable lines of a warrior called to action.

“What family?” she stuttered.

“My mother.”

She tried to absorb that. All this time together, and except for the odd reference to a bad childhood, she had not even been aware his mother was still alive. In fact, the afternoon that he had arrived at her apartment shortly after the kitchen fire, she was positive he had *implied* his mother was deceased. She felt the shock of him blocking that part of his life from her.

"I have to go."

But her sense of loss and recrimination needed to be put aside for the time being. He looked so shattered. He looked as if, whatever this was, he should not be alone with it.

"I'm coming with you."

He started to shake his head, but she could see he was rattled, that he both wanted her support and didn't. She scrambled off the counter and went and changed quickly, her evening as a princess as over as if she was Cinderella, midnight had come and she had turned back into the ordinary girl she really was.

His steps were long and urgent as he shepherded Bree outside. In their rush to get into her apartment, he had forgotten to dismiss the limo, and it idled at the curb waiting for him. Now, they got in and he gave his own address. There they switched to one of his own cars, ignoring the soulful sounds of Beau, from inside the house, crying that he knew they were home.

The car Brand chose from his six-bay garage was an Italian four-door Maserati, but it might as well have been a pumpkin for how the magic had drained from the evening. He was silent and grim, barely acknowledging her as he scrolled through his phone, looking something up with urgency.

And then they were driving through the seediest part of Vancouver, streets lined with dilapidated buildings with people huddled in the doorways.

He stopped in front of one. It was a no-parking zone, but he ignored that. A sandwich board announced Tonight and Tonight Only, Elvis Impersonations.

He was storming through the door, Bree hard on his heels.

The room was dark, and had only a smattering of people sitting at tables. It smelled bad, of smoke and spilled beer.

The stage was illuminated, though, and an Elvis gyrated across it, belting out "Hound Dog."

He *did* remind Bree of that horrible man she had met on e-Us.

She looked at Brand, arms folded across his chest, as he scanned the tables. The performance, the club and the Elvis impersonators sitting around waiting for their turns might have been funny in an absurd way, particularly coming from the ball to this, but it was not funny. Bree glanced at Brand's face. She was not sure she had ever seen such terrible torment in one person's expression before in her life.

He spotted something and moved across the dark room. Bree, not sure what to do, or what exactly was going on, followed.

Brand slid into a chair at a table occupied by a lovely woman with gray hair. She turned and smiled at him, put her arm on his sleeve, then turned back to the music, rapt. Brand, though he hardly seemed to know Bree was there, pulled out the chair beside him and nodded at it. Bree took it.

The song ended with blessed abruptness, as if someone, having suffered quite enough, had pulled the plug on the karaoke machine.

"I'm glad you called me, Mom," Brand said quietly into the sudden silence.

Mom.

"I was trying to get up my nerve to go on," his mother said, and then, her voice sad, she added, "But it's not me anymore, is it?"

"Maybe not," he said gently.

"But don't throw out my posters just yet!"

Her posters. All this time, Brand could have told Bree, but nothing. Not a single word, even though there had been opportunities.

"Hello," his mother said softly, noticing Bree. "I'm Diana. I used to do a great Elvis impression."

Almost shyly she took a bag out from under the table and spilled its contents out for Bree to see. She fingered the white, metal-studded fabric almost lovingly.

"I was good, wasn't I, Brand?" she asked, her tone wistful.

"Yeah, Mom," he said. "You were good."

Bree's mind felt tumultuous as snippets of conversations came back to her. *Somehow I didn't figure you for an Elvis kind of guy. What's your favorite Elvis song? Must I pick only one? Impossible.*

"Bree," Brand said, his flinty eyes intent on her face, "meet my mother."

Bree looked to him, and then to the woman. She extended her hand. "Mrs. Wallace?" she said uncertainly. "My pleasure. Bree Evans."

"Diana."

Lively eyes, dark like his, scanned her face, a certain shrewdness in them. "I suppose I should go home now?"

"I think that's a good idea, Mom."

They left and he put his mother in the front seat, and Bree took the back. They drove through the city in complete silence to a lovely building, which, even in all its loveliness, was clearly some sort of institution.

"I'll call you a cab," Brand said grimly.

"I'll wait," Bree said, just as grimly.

He looked as if he might argue, but his mother got out of the car, and looked as if she might be considering going anywhere but in. The weariness on his face was heartbreaking, and he just lifted a shoulder, got out, put his hand on his mother's shoulder and guided her to the main door.

It was nearly an hour before he came out.

His face was gray with exhaustion. He slid into the seat beside her.

"I'm sorry I took so long," he said. "She was quite agitated. I stayed with her for a while until she settled. It's an assisted-living place, not a jail. My mother's bipolar, with schizophrenic tendencies."

He sounded like a doctor, clinical, rhyming off facts.

"The medication takes away her upswing, and the voices. She misses both. She can be very good at hiding the fact she isn't taking her medication. I probably should have picked up on it."

Bree heard self-recrimination there. He'd been too involved with her. It had distracted him.

"I'll drive you home now. There was no need for you to wait." They drove away.

She knew he had no intention of coming in, that the moment was gone, possibly forever.

She knew he was tired. But it still had to be said. "You don't think we have things to discuss?"

"Must we?"

"Yes. Why didn't you tell me, Brand? Why didn't you trust me with this?"

He was silent. They pulled up in front of her building. He nodded to the door, as if he expected her just to get out!

"You let me believe your mother was dead."

He looked truly astonished by that. "What?"

"That day at my apartment, when we were drinking the cheap wine, you said she would have considered it champagne. *Would have.* Past tense."

"Because she doesn't drink anymore, not because she's dead!"

"All this time you could have said something. Anything. That day in the kayak, I asked you about you and Elvis, I said I got the impression you didn't like Elvis that much. Some might say a perfect segue for you to tell me about your mom. But no. Nothing. Not a word."

"Pardon me for not revealing all my secrets to you." His voice was cold.

"But I revealed all mine to you, Brand," she reminded him softly. "I told you about my baby. I shared my deepest loss with you. I trusted you with it."

She thought this reminder of her own vulnerability would soften him, but his silence was cold. It made her more grimly determined to have her say.

"It's not that your mother is ill that hurts," she told him. Her tone was quiet, but she was not sure she had ever felt so angry. "It's that you didn't trust me to do the right thing with it. To be the right person."

Again, he was silent for a long time, and when he turned to her, her heart stopped beating, and her breath stopped the steady rise and fall of life. What she saw in his eyes was an unfathomable coldness. Cruelty.

She saw everything had changed. She saw he would not see her again.

"No," he said harshly, "I didn't trust you with it. Goodbye, Bree."

Stunned, she got out of the car. In a moment of fury, she slammed the door so hard his car rocked. Still, he did not squeal away. She wished he would have. Instead, he waited to make sure she got to the door. She kept her shoulders straight, her spine proud, as she put in her door code. It was as he drove away that she dissolved, and let the first tears fall.

All this time, she realized, she had given more and more and more trust to him.

And he had given her none in return. He had not even trusted her to be understanding about his mother's fragile, broken condition.

Had he not known her at all?

"All men are rotten," she decided furiously. "All of them!"

Brand drove away after he saw Bree was safely inside her building. He felt sick for what he had just said to her, that he didn't trust her with it.

The truth was, he had not trusted himself with it.

He had allowed himself to be distracted from the truth of his life, to pretend that he could have what other people had.

He had allowed that dangerous thing called hope to creep into his world.

This is what Brand had managed to avoid facing after the enchantment of the last month—that he brought a long and horrible history with him, running down his line from two sides. A selfish man who had such a cold heart he had abandoned his wife and, worse, his son.

And then his mother, his poor long-suffering mother, who would sometimes get better for long periods of time, only to fall back into her delusions, an intensifying of her obsession with Elvis usually providing the first red flag that she had abandoned her medication, that she missed the "ups" and missed the "voices."

But this time, he hadn't noticed. He'd been too busy. Selfish and cold, just like his father.

This is what he knew for sure.

He loved Bree Evans with a love that nearly took his breath away. He loved how funny she was and how brave. He loved how she made the most ordinary of things shine as if they were lit from within. He loved the wonder in her face when he invited her into a world where money could buy anything, and her equal wonder over a dog romping joyously through a mud puddle. He loved her loyalty and her creativity and how smart and how inventive she was. He loved how she had hope.

This is what he'd forgotten that day he had decided that she could not hurt him. This is what he had so selfishly put aside: that he could hurt her. That's what he had forgotten in that totally self-centered moment of *wanting* what he had seen shining in her.

All the things he had never had: a safe harbor, future children laughing.

She deserved those things. The truth was this: both conditions his mother had could be inherited. If he had either, they would have shown up by now. But that did not make his children safe.

Is that what his father had thought, when he walked away and never come back? That he could barely deal with one person with mental-health issues? What if his son had those issues, too?

Brand could not bear it if he was the one who crushed in Bree, for all time, those things that mattered so much to her. How could he create the kind of home she'd enjoyed as a child? How would he learn those skills when he had never experienced the security and stability of a good home? Nothing in living in a car, and stealing creamers from fast-food restaurants, and walking in the door, listening to see what Elvis song his mother had on so he could judge her mood, had prepared him for the kind of life Bree desired so desperately and deserved so richly.

Really, the most loving thing he could ever do for her?

He had just done it.

He had said goodbye. Not just for tonight. Forever. It had felt as if he was ripping his own heart out saying that to her, keeping his face cold and cruel in the light of her hurt and her wanting and her hope. Especially her hope.

As he drove away through the rain-filled night,

it felt as if he had entered a pit of impenetrable blackness such as he had never known before, and in a way he welcomed it, like a man facing his absolute reality and coming home to the place he'd always known that he belonged.

CHAPTER FIFTEEN

BREE WOKE UP the morning after the ball knowing exactly how Cinderella had felt. She had *almost* had it all. And then, at the ring of a clock at midnight—or the quack of a phone, as the case might be—it had been snatched away from her. She was lying in her bed waiting for that familiar despair to creep over her, to steal her breath and her strength and her desire to get up.

Instead, as she was lying there, scanning her feelings, she was pleasantly surprised that she didn't feel despair at all. She felt really, really angry.

"All men are rotten," she repeated to herself. She liked it. It would be her new mantra!

She got up and looked in the mirror in her bathroom. Her eyes were ringed with black from last night's cry, but as she washed up, she was aware she was done crying, and that she had something very important to do.

She dressed in slim-fitting jeans and a plain cotton blouse, and then threw her beautiful new cloak over top. She filled up Oliver's water and food dishes, then she put on sneakers to drive, but put her red stilettos in the backseat.

And then she drove. She thought she would have second thoughts on the long drive, lose her courage or her nerve, but neither happened. If anything, her confidence grew. She had a sense that this was something she should have done a long, long time ago.

She drove through the familiar campus. It was summer session, but there was still lots of life. She noticed the girls, in particular, looking so carefree, so filled with hope for their futures.

She had been that girl once. She had *allowed* Paul Weston to steal that from her. But here was the part that filled her with shame: had her silence allowed him to steal it from other young women, as well?

The new her parked in the spot reserved for

visiting VIPs, and she changed shoes. The new Bree walked right by the president of the university's stammering secretary, knocked briefly on his door and went in.

He looked up, surprised, and she let the door swing shut behind her.

Twenty minutes later, with assurances of a complete investigation, she strode across the campus in her heels. She felt like a warrior: she could feel the absolute confidence shimmering around her, like a crackle of electricity in the air before a coming storm.

Men stopped and stared at her as if she was the most ravishing woman they had ever seen. Some of them ventured a smile. Women seemed to know she was on a mission for all of them, because they smiled at her as though they recognized her, or recognized something in her that they liked.

She didn't even hesitate at the familiar steps of the culinary arts building. The heels did not even slow her down.

She went in and stopped by the lecture hall.

And there he was. She could see him through the small rectangular glass frame that looked in to the hall.

He was dressed as he always had been: a tweedy jacket and rumpled pants. Today he was sporting an ascot. She could clearly see he was wearing the costume of a distracted, artsy college professor.

She took a deep breath and opened the door. All eyes were on her as she went down the sloping aisle, past the rows of theater-style seats, up the three stairs to the raised dais he stood on.

"Paul, do you remember me?" she asked, her voice loud and clear.

His eyes wide, the man who had haunted her nightmares looked at her. His mouth opened, then closed, opened again.

"Bree," he said, "I'm in the middle of—"

She saw what she had never seen as his eyes shifted away from hers. The weakness and the cowardice, a man who had used his position and power to feed his own sick needs.

"I don't care what you're in the middle of," she

said, and she turned to face his students. She took a deep breath, and began.

"I want to tell you about a young girl, who sat right where you are sitting now," she said. There was no hesitation and no fear. "Her father had just died."

"Bree." His voice was plaintive.

"Paul, sit down and shut up."

He stared at her. He scuttled over to a chair and sat down.

She finished her story. For a moment, there was shocked silence. For a moment, she wondered if she had done the right thing. And then one lone, brave young woman stood. Bree could see tears running down her face. She began to clap. And then another rose, and another. The young women were the first, but the young men followed. She turned to look at Paul. His chair was empty.

And then she was surrounded in a sea of caring.

Strangers who felt as if they were not strangers at all were hugging her, some of the girls were telling her about the creepy moves Paul had put on them.

Bree realized she felt as if she was leaving her body, as if she had floated way up above herself and was looking down at the woman in the stiletto heels and the red cape, and seeing her for what she was.

Brave enough, finally, to be worthy of the gift called love.

Days later, she did not feel quite so brave. She felt worn down from emotion, and her devastating sense of loss. Her mantra was not strong enough to carry her, and didn't even seem true anymore.

How did "all men are rotten" fit into being worthy of the gift that was love? It didn't. Her father had not been rotten. And Brand was not rotten, either.

He was human.

She thought of the look in Brand's eyes the last night she had seen him. She had mistaken it for coldness and cruelty and rejection.

But now, having seen Paul Weston again, she was very aware of what those things looked like. And Brand had none of them in him. None.

What she had seen in his eyes was the lonely bleakness of a man who thought he had to protect her, even if that meant from himself.

Bree realized she had to use all this newfound bravery to go into his dark world and bring him to safety. She had to be brave enough to go after him. To go after Brand, a man who had only ever used his position and his power for good. A man who was as worthy of her as she was of him.

He just didn't know it yet.

But when she called his cell, there was no answer. When she called his office, she was told he was not available.

The new Bree put on her bravery cloak, and went downtown. She had a cookie contract after all. There was no reason not to drop by his office!

For once, there was a receptionist at the front desk in that luxurious front foyer. No joyous dog came bounding out the door.

"I need to see Mr. Wallace," Bree said.

The receptionist looked at her, and obviously recognized her. Bree had been a bit of a fixture for the past month. Was there the faint pity of one not unfamiliar with the heartsick trying to get through to her boss in her tone?

"I'm afraid he's out of the country at the moment. I'll tell him you called by?"

"Out of the country? But when will he be back?"

"I'm not at liberty to say that."

Bree wanted to leap across the desk, place her hands around that skinny throat and squeeze an answer from her. What country? How long would he be gone?

"I think he's going to be away for some time," the receptionist said, and now she looked genuinely sad.

"Where's Beau?"

"He's out of the country, too."

Bree felt a wave of relief. "Thank goodness," she murmured. Beau, the only one he trusted completely with his heart, was with him.

She turned to leave. The door that separated the office space from the front entrance swung open.

A young man walked out. She recognized him from his beard, and from her first day here, when he had been swinging on that hammock, throwing a beanbag in the air.

It niggled her memory. *He is one guy I make sure to talk to every single day.*

“Kevin?” she said.

He turned and looked at her absently.

She racked her memory for the afternoon that she and Brand had practiced phrases out of the Klingon language, laughing until they could laugh no more.

Klingons, Brand had told her gravely, did not have greetings per se, but still she drew a phrase from her memory.

She tentatively tried out the crazy sounding mix of consonants and vowels. She must have done something right.

Kevin brightened instantly. He responded with the same mix.

Literally, it meant “what do you want?”

“I want to take you for coffee,” she said. The receptionist had been watching the whole interchange. When Bree glanced back at her, she had ducked her head, but she was smiling.

CHAPTER SIXTEEN

IT WAS A life out of a dream, Brand told himself, as he shook seawater from his hair and tucked his surfboard under his arm.

He had his dog, he had the ocean. He had spectacular sunsets, and day after day of sunshine. The palm trees were swaying gently in a tropical breeze. Up the beach was a cottage, completely open-air, with state-of-the-art electronics, so he could check in with the office and talk to his mother.

Unfortunately, the sand was everywhere, golden and unending.

And it was the very same color as Bree's hair.

Unfortunately, even though he was having the life out of a dream, it was not a dream he would wish on anyone.

He had never been plagued with loneliness before, and now he awoke with it as his companion and slept with it at night.

Even Beau was aware something was amiss. Instead of following him exuberantly into the water, snapping at waves he could never catch, he laid on shore, watching, lethargic, sadness coming out of every pore and stinky wrinkle.

Except right now, Beau's ears were perked up. His great head was lifted off his paws, and he was staring at the line of palm trees along the edge of the beach.

Suddenly he gave a woof, heaved himself up and began to gallop along the beach toward the trees.

Someone was coming. A woman.

As she got closer, he saw her hair. It couldn't be. But he had thought no one else in the world had hair like that.

He wasn't tormented enough? Out in the middle of nowhere a woman with the same hair was coming toward him? A woman with a colorful wraparound skirt knotted at a slender waist, wearing a black bikini top.

His heart rose as she got closer.

It couldn't be. It was a mirage, a man dying of thirst in the desert imagining the only thing that could save him.

The dog reached her, and she went down on one knee.

There was only one person his dog greeted like that. Brand wanted to run to her, just like the dog, to throw himself in a delirious pile of joy at her feet.

But he could not.

He needed to be strong. Stronger than he had ever been in his life.

For the love of her, for the love of Bree Evans, he needed to be strong.

He forced himself not to go to her. Instead, he wrapped a towel around his waist, dropped down into his hammock, put on his sunglasses and picked up a book.

"Brand?"

He lowered his sunglasses and peered at her over the rim. He pretended surprise, and then irritation.

"What are you doing here? Nobody knows I'm here."

"Kevin does."

"No, he doesn't."

"Well, he's a geek. He traced a telephone ping or something."

"Why would he do that?"

"He'd do anything for a woman who speaks Klingon."

"Which you don't," Brand said with a snort.

"You'd be surprised what love is willing to do to find its way."

Love. He snapped his sunglasses back over his eyes, nestled deeper in his hammock, looked intently at his book. He hoped it wasn't upside down.

"You've wasted your time," he said. "I don't want to see you. Go away."

"I'm not going away."

He hazarded a look at her, frowned and looked away hastily. There was something new in her. A strength, a self-certainty that she had not had before.

He contemplated that. He was falling to pieces here on his desert-island dream world with his dog. And she was…what? Blossoming? Coming into herself?

She was more gorgeous than she had ever been and she'd been plenty gorgeous.

A bikini! That said it all, really. Over a month ago, she'd been a one-piece kind of girl. He glanced at her again. He wanted to touch her hair. It was the *exact* color of the sand. He glared at the book.

"Do you want to know what I've learned over the past few weeks, Brand?"

"Not particularly," he said. He deliberately licked his finger and turned a page of the book.

She shoved the hammock. It rocked wildly and he thought he was going to get dumped in the sand. He managed to extricate himself and find his feet.

He stood looking down at her. She gazed up at him with those soulful, earnest eyes. Those soulful earnest eyes that had a new layer to them.

Bravery.

The kind of bravery a man who did not feel brave could cling to, like a life raft was going by just as he had resigned himself to drowning.

"Humph," he said, annoyed with himself.

She lifted an eyebrow, as if she could *see* right through him.

"This is what I learned about myself," she said with that quiet new confidence. "I thought love had broken me once. After Paul, after the baby."

Did she have to mention that? It made it hard to be mean to her, to do what needed to be done to drive her away. No, not hard—impossible.

"But now I see that's not true at all. What broke me was an imitation of love. Real love is different."

He stared at her. He could feel himself swimming toward the paddle she was holding out, even as he ordered himself to swim away from her, to choose the loneliness of an endless sea.

"Real love doesn't break people," she said. "Real love is like the love I received from my family. It filled me with hope and it made me a promise that good would always outweigh bad."

"Naive," he growled. But she put her fingers on his lips. Her touch was a balm to his tormented soul. He could not do anything now but listen, even though he knew he was touching the paddle she was holding out.

"Love, genuine love, makes you stronger. It gives you a belief in yourself and the world. It makes you more authentic, not less."

He was silent, but inwardly he could feel the slow tremble of complete surrender.

"You think," she said softly, "that you will be like your father, but you have already shown in every way that you are in the world that you are not. He ran away from your mother, and responsibility.

"You have embraced those things."

"Speaking of my mother, there's a chance it's genetic—"

"Shh," she said. "You think I don't know that's the fear you've wrestled with your whole life? Brand, you already know so much more about love than you have ever given yourself credit for.

"Love—the kind that sticks with it through the

hard stuff—you already know that. That's what has made you who you are. That's what has made me love you so helplessly. So hopelessly."

"Look, I tried this. The love stuff. It's not for me. I warned you. Wendy. Lasted three days, I—"

"Shh." There it was again. Gentle. But a command.

"I'm not saying you aren't scared of love," Bree said. "I'm not saying that at all. Why else would such a smart man pick such a perfectly ill-matched person as Wendy?

"You're scared of it. You've seen the power it has to wound.

"But what I've seen? I've seen the power it has to make a man like you, who is so *good*, so decent, so courageous, despite the wound."

In his mind, he could see himself heaving himself into her lifeboat.

She felt his absolute surrender the moment it happened. Her arms went around him. She held him with astonishing strength. He could feel the strong beat of her heart, and the tenderness of her skin.

"I love you," she said. "And I'm going to love you until my very last breath. I am never, as long as I live, going to stop."

He let those words ease into him, ease past all his defenses, ease over his walls, something warm and fluid, that could not be stopped by something so small as one man's desire to shield others from the possible pain of this force.

"What about my children?" he asked, and he could hear the anguish in his own voice.

And she could hear it, too.

"What blessings they will be to the world," she said quietly. "What blessings our children—loved and accepted for all their strengths and all their flaws—will be to the world."

He took her face between both his hands and searched it for any trace of fear, for any trace of a lie.

But he saw what he had always seen in her face, even when she was a young girl going to her senior prom.

He saw that her gift to the world was hope.

Belief.

A tremendous unshakable conviction.

And that conviction was that love would always win. It was even stronger in her now than it had been then, when she was a young girl who had never had one bad thing happen to her.

Now, she had had bad things happen to her. She had suffered tremendous losses.

And still, she stood before him, unshakable in her faith, stronger than ever.

The word came from somewhere deep within him. It was his soul recognizing what she had held out to him. It was his soul yearning for a place to rest, for a place he had never had.

It was his soul, his heart, his mind, his whole being accepting the invitation she had held out to him.

To be brave.

To step into the unknown.

To have hope.

To believe.

To embrace the greatest force in the entire universe—love.

"Yes," he whispered to each of those things, and then, his voice stronger, to her he said, "Yes."

And then stronger still, even though this time it was just within himself, it felt as if he was shouting it to the earth and the waves and the trees, and the stars, shouting it with all the joy and strength it deserved—yes.

CHAPTER SEVENTEEN

THE GARDEN LOOKED the way it had always meant to look. Pails of white flowers—begonias, Brand vaguely thought—flanked the back steps, and peeked out from every shaded corner of his backyard.

The house looked different. Every window was open and so were the French doors. Analytically, he knew the house had not changed. It was the same color, there had been no renovations.

And yet, everything felt different, as if the house was happy, and as if its happiness was spilling out those open doors and windows.

The clatter of people busy in the kitchen and a shout of laughter reached him.

His back garden was filled with chairs with white satin bows on them, and people milled around, filling the space with color and energy and laughter and a shared belief in happy endings.

Given Vancouver's weather, it was a miracle it was not raining today, but there you had it.

Brand was a man who had come to believe in miracles.

Bree could have had the wedding anywhere. In a different country, on a beach, in the best hotel in Vancouver, but she had looked surprised when he had asked her where she would like to become his wife.

"At home, of course," she said. "That's where your mom will be most comfortable, and then Beau can be part of our celebration, too. Even Oliver can be part of our day."

Sure enough, Oliver was peeping sourly out from under one of those pails of begonias. They had been adjusting the cat to his new home for several weeks now. He had taken to it—and to bossing around Beau—with a kind of regal disdain that Brand had learned meant he was almost deliriously happy.

He considered that word. Home. In the last few

months, his house had been transformed into a home. Bree had not moved in. She had wanted to. He had refused her. And he had refused her desire to seal their relationship physically as well.

He had almost given in to that temptation the night of his company's charity ball. Now, he sometimes wondered about that. If the intervention hadn't been divine.

Because that was not what he wanted with Bree.

He wanted to be the man she deserved, the man her father had always expected he would be. A man who would cherish her and treat her with complete honor, always.

So, here he was, minutes before his wedding, contemplating the nature of miracles and divine intervention. He was a changed man from what he had been just a few months ago.

Then, he had mistakenly thought he had everything. Then, he had thought he was wealthy.

"Time to go, buddy."

Chelsea's man, Reed, tapped him on the shoulder. He and Bree had become so close to the other couple, who had begun dating almost as soon as

Reed submitted his findings on the fire to the investigating team.

An electrical fire.

No one to blame.

A faulty circuit.

Or a miracle. One that had brought this young couple, obviously made for each other, together.

Just as a last-minute decision to go to that gala had reunited Brand with Bree.

Brand walked up the aisle of chairs to the back of his yard, where a flower-bedecked trellis had been erected. Reed flanked him on his right and Beau padded along beside him, looking as pleased as his wrinkly face would allow. Beau's white ribbon was already somewhat bedraggled.

People began to drift to the chairs.

Brand's mother took her seat in the front row, looking beautiful in a pink two-piece suit that Bree had helped her choose. She radiated the soft glow of wellness. Elvis was banished, for now. Brand dared not hope forever, but there was something about watching Bree with his mother that made his throat close and his eyes sting.

Bree treated his mother with an unfathomable tenderness that his mother reacted to like a parched plant that had needed rain. Brand knew love couldn't heal her, or else his already would have, and yet there was something about the steadiness of Bree's love that brought out the best in his mother, that brought out a side of her he had never seen.

He'd asked Bree once how she loved his mother so completely, and she had seemed so genuinely surprised by the question.

"She's part of you," she had said. "She's part of everything that is best about you—your strength and your decency and your drive. I love her for what she gave you, and I love her for her innate bravery. And I love her for the way she sees the world."

Bree's own mother, came and sat by his, and their hands found each other, two women who knew there was a certain kind of bitter sweetness to saying goodbye to one kind of relationship with their children, and hello to another one.

The music started. No Elvis, there was no

sense testing his mother's newfound equilibrium with that.

No, it was the soaring and falling notes of Pachelbel's Canon.

The chatter quieted, and a hush fell over the filled seats, letting the music fill the garden area of the yard.

First, Chelsea came out. She was beautiful in a short aquamarine dress. Brand glanced at Reed beside him, and saw everything he felt for Bree in that other man's face.

Chelsea, like Bree, had come in to herself, and she radiated the quiet confidence of a woman well-loved.

A hush fell over the back garden as Bree stepped out of the house and slowly came down the steps. At her side was her stepfather, Mike.

Brand had to swallow, and then swallow hard again.

He had never seen a woman as beautiful as his soon-to-be wife.

The dress, of course, was exquisite. Her sunshine-on-sand hair was up, and threaded with flowers, her shoulders were bare, and the dress fit tight to her slender form, and then flared out at her waist in a cloud of white that floated around her and behind her.

But it was not the dress that stole the breath from him. Bree was so radiant she put the sun to shame. Everything in the garden faded: the music, the flowers, the guests, their mothers, her stepfather on her arm. Everything faded, until it was just her. Until the whole world was just her.

Coming toward him, with the entire future shining in her clear eyes.

* * * * *